Intergalactic Trouble in Lit Manchester

(Or The Unexpected Virtue the Face of the End of the World)

To request permissions, contact the publisher at
ollyjrnuttall@gmail.com

ISBN: 9798595876797
Hardcover: 1
Paperbook: 2
Semi tough cover: 3
Audiobook: 4
Ediblebook: 55378008

First paperback edition January 2021

Edited by O. J. R. Nuttall (hence all the unspotted errors)
Cover art by Ines Funke
Title Graphics: Melanie Tamiazzo
Layout by Oliver Nuttall
Photographs by G. O. Ogle
Theme Music: Ol Nuttall and Jimmy Nail

Printed by HP Desk Jet 2710

Never mind the B(Ol)logs
If you can find him, maybe you can hire the Ol Team
Some Dull suburb in Manchester
UK
Europe
Earth
Milky Way
Web Address: https://ollyjrnuttall.wixsite.com/website

Acknowledgements

So many people to thank, so little space (no pun intended) to do it. Obviously, my thanks go my amazing family - my dad and Ed (for so many influences from you both), Em, Jess and Sam and all the weird rag tag family present, past and future. Extra special and unlimited thanks to my mum who always encouraged and supported me to go in whatever weird direction worked for me, I'll never ever have enough words of gratitude for all you've done for me mum.

Thanks to all my friends (I hope you know who you all are, cos if I list you all the word count is going to rocket up) who have supported/inspired me in ways you may, or may not be aware of, special thanks to The Bens, Ste, Lat, Nick, Paul, Sam, Kate, Hayles. And big thanks to the following people who have read parts of this book, and/or my other writing, and were kind enough not to call it total shite; Ben H, Hayles, Ines, Nic, Lizzie, John M, Paul C, Rek, Ben C, Di, Emily, Nick, Bex, Chiharu, Shanta.

A massive thanks to the amazingly talented Ines Funke for creating the front cover, if nothing else the book looks amazing and has proved the maxim that you can't polish a turd, but you can roll it in glitter.

I hope the book gives you a few laughs, some entertainment and a bit of a breather from the world and failing that you have gained some kindling (unless ironically you bought the kindle version) for a fire or toilet paper (and definitely don't use your kindle for that).

And to anyone who said to me "you should write this stuff down", this book is your fault.

Thanks for coming this far with me.

For Jess and Sam

Prologue

Come ye sit closer and listen to my story, closer, closer, no not on my knee, it's not that kind of story. Yes, that bean bag should be enough if you lower yourself gently in. I cannot guarantee you will escape its perilous grasp so easily.

My story? It's about everything, life, love, existence, trout fishing with dynamite and Gnu tossing, however I'm not here to tell you about my story. I'm here to tell you the story for the ages, about the quest for an item of such power, such vast potential, such fell abilities that it could, that it could…sorry I got distracted by a squirrel…what was I talking about again?

Oh yeah that glove thingy, yeah that. Well, let me tell you about that, in the control of the wrong person, it could destroy the foundations of the universe, or at the least give them foundations a ruddy good shake; this story is the quest for the rubber glove of power[1].

So, let me begin this tail (spelling mistakes and all) of rollicking adventure and swashbuklery and introduce you to our humble hero called…wait what's their name…hang on let me check my book, I've bent the corner of the relevant page…oh nuts I've left my copy of the story on the train.

---

[1] Other better names for this item are available for a small fee.

Not a problem, I can give you the abridged version via the medium of interpretive dance. Wait where are you going….

Well, that's the dynamic, grab the reader's attention introduction buggered.

Space Maps

Editor's note; These are random pictures of space so I've no idea of the accuracy of the arrows. Some smart arse has probably figured out where abouts in space the photos are actually of and will pull me up on my inaccuracies. Let me tell you this brother, if you think this photo is highly inaccurate and taking liberties, wait until you get into the book proper…

Part of the intention of this book was to put Sale on the map, I think this may be taking things a little too literally.

Cast, Characters, Dramatis Personae, Protagonists, Antagonists, Heroes and Villains, People who crop up in the story, Extras, Stunt Doubles, Animal Trainers, Puppeteers

Any characters in this story are fictional, and any similarities with people past and present are entirely coincidental. If you find you are like any of the character in this story then Jesus, how two dimensional and badly written is your personality?

Character names are liable to change when the author comes up with better ones or forgets what he called the character earlier in the story, your mortgage payments may go up as well as down, get plenty of vitamin D, be nice to people, don't eat yellow snow.

Barry Ostlethwaite:

The most feared bounty hunter in the known universe, four black holes and a couple of corners in a shopping precinct yet to be discovered.

He is powerful. He is without mercy. He takes no prisoners. He has no sense of direction. No really, he was once hired as a mercenary in the battle of Little Big Trombone. He arrived late and utterly wiped out the robo-turkey army, before realising he was facing the wrong way and had actually been hired by the robo-turkey army. To this day, he is still barred from all intergalactic branches of Kentucky Fried Robo-turkey (which is a shame for him, as he was a big fan of their Steel Giblet burger with peri peri oil – mmm tasty), although this ban has probably added four years to his life expectancy.

Barry is Terran bus driver[2] and hales from Barnsley (hence the ridiculously stereotyped name). Out on a fishing trip one day, he accidently stumbled through an inter-dimensional warp gate someone had left open in the public toilets (careless, but it happens) and ended up transported to the planet Buckfast[3]. Unqualified to drive the turbo-hyper-super-ok bus on the planet, he went to see the careers adviser at Buckfast Jobcentre. After waiting four light years to be seen by a Jobcentre Work Coach he decided becoming a Self-Employed bounty hunter was preferable to sitting any longer on a sofa that smelt a little of poo[4].

As this fell bounty hunter, he has taken part in one interdimensional battle, three infinity wars, a drunken skirmish, a bit of handbags and one thumb war to the death. His most famous battle was against the intergalactic taxman, for submitting a late expenses return. Despite employing an anti-matter death ray against the

---

[2] The lack of direction really should have put him off being a bus driver, but he's a stubborn idiot. Passengers know to pack meals and changes of clothes if Barry is driving the bus. Also being a bus driver, he has immaculate timing for moving away just as people get close to the bus doors.
[3] Not a health drink kind of planet.
[4] There are many worrying explanations for why it smelt thus.

tax office, he ultimately had to surrender to their superior admin skills.

Tiring of the all the killing, maiming and having a sore thumb, Barry aims to do one last big job, pay off the taxman and retire to play zero gravity Jenga (which lacks the intrinsic peril of the standard gravity version) and knit slightly rude woolen caricatures of the cast of the (inexplicably) popular TV show The Good Life.

The fates may yet cast Barry a vital role in this tale, but probably not, as you know what those fates are like, a proper fickle bunch.

To this day he is number seven in the Jobcentre queue.

Magic Suzie:

Residing from the dimension Izzywhizzyletsgetbusydonia[5], the centre of the universe for the most powerful magic creatures, wizards, wannabe warlocks, witches, Wizbits and amateur conjurers (who've no chance of having any real power until they start calling themselves something that begins with the letter 'W').

---

[5] A name that the planet regularly has a referendum on, because A. Its Crap, and B. Sign writers all end up with Carpel Tunnel Syndrome

Suzie is a humanoid magician rated the most powerful in 'magic rhombus'[6] Top Trumps. She also has a 4-star Uber rating and a dog licence.

Suzie's magic is based entirely around light entertainment tricks. For example, in the 48-minute War (casualties, 0.3 humans and an allotment growing cauliflower), Suzie pulled a rabbit out of her hat to ward off the Cheesy Wotsit Orks from the planet Blowdonia. However, this was no ordinary rabbit, this was a thirty foot rabbit with a hangover and armed with a plank of wood with a nail in it. The resulting battle has featured in four songs, a couple of films and as a promotional wrapper on a Gregg's Vegan steak slice.

Despite such power, no one ever gave Suzie the hoary old 'with great power comes great responsibility' chat. As a consequence, she is exceptionally sunny in her outlook. Even when facing off the Bollock Demon from the Phil Collins dimension, she takes it in her cheery stride.

She is also very chatty and has actually talked the hind legs off a donkey. To be fair, the donkey was looking to sell them as he wanted to replace them with 20-foot electro wheels so he could enter the Le Ass 24 hours race[7] Suzie

---

[6] Because obviously magicians need a shadowy members club to protect themselves even thought they can, you know, do magic and stuff.

[7] Postscript, the donkey came 9th in the race and retired to paint challenging abstract art of the actress June Whitfield. Ron Howard is currently in talks to blandly direct his biopic.

now uses the donkey legs to win regularly at Wizard Twister[8].

Suzie is sworn protector of the universe, a role she carries out with a smile, because she sees it as a jolly wheeze and also as she has a PA, Noble Derek, to do all her paperwork.

Noble Derek:

Suzie's PA. Not featuring in this story.

HA'Lith'Ngal'Llanfair'Sfar'loadashite[9] (pronounced Luci, with 2 Cs):

Luci is part of a shadowy[10] cabal of assassins[11] who live in a caravan site just outside an inter dimensional version of Fleetwood[12]. These assassins have a code they absolutely adhere to. But much like the highway code after passing your driving test, none of them fully remember what the code actually is and they certainly don't remember the breaking distance in dagger length, for when you thrust a knife at someone.

---

[8] Same as regular Twister, but you also have to place your beard on a corresponding colour. Women magicians have argued for centuries that the game is inherently sexist.

[9] Her birth certificate is on A2 paper – rare.

[10] They're always shadowy, you never get a sunny cabal, do you?

[11] Well, they say they're shadowy in their Mission Statement, but they advertise in the yellow pages under A for Assassins. They're still annoyed at Aaron A Aardvark Assassin Extraordinaire (and bouncy castle lender) for getting in front of them in the phone book,

[12] Much like the regular Fleetwood albeit much further away which is probably preferable.

These assassins' practice Threestoogejitsu a lethal form of martial arts built entirely around slapstick violence from early Hollywood movies. Luci thoroughly enjoys the violence, but on the whole would rather be eating ice creams and doing cartwheels. She has a soft spot for Aardman animations, especially Shaun the Sheep. She has yet to employ any of these pleasures into her missions but remains optimistic they'll be needed to stop the forces of evil one day.

Although Luci feigns not having time for anyone, she actually enjoys the company of people, though she always struggles to show it, using violence as a means of expressing her emotions[13]. She has recently taken up water colouring as a method of reconciling her blood thirsty training with expressing herself. Her first piece was called '101 ways to injure someone with a rubber duck'. The Tate Modern is considering her application.

Luci hates the term 'banter' and will clip anyone who uses it as an excuse for rampant sexism, homophobia, xenophobia[14] around the ear. Unfortunately, given her training, Luci doesn't know her own strength and her clips have been known to take peoples ears clean off. Those ears that do survive often need intense physiotherapy and weeks of counselling to recover.

---

[13] Like a rugby player, but with less homoeroticism.
[14] The kind of person who says, "I'm not racist but..." and then proves you can disregard all the words before the 'but'.

Luci struggles to understand the concept of how an assassin, who let's face it has 'mostly killing people for money' on their job description also offer themselves out for heroic services. It's a crazy conflicted world she reasons, and doesn't ponder on it much more than that.

Zed Turpin:

They call him the sage. They call him the mysterious. They call him the enigma. They call him, you know, that bloke we saw in the middle of the road shouting at cars the other day, whatsis name?!

Zed is scholarly, very scholarly. There isn't a book or film he hasn't read the synopsis of[15]. If there was a film version of this book he would be played by Ian McKellen, or Patrick Stewart, or the ghost of Sid James.

Zed has a beard that screams academia, which can land him in a lot of trouble in the quiet section of a train or library. He strokes his beard as he ponders an answer to a question. Some feel he enters a trance state where knowledge syphons through his body, though more likely he is just buying time as he tries to subtly look up the answer on the computer he has stashed in his face fuzz.

He has been known to take as long as three weeks to answer a question, which is a

---

[15] And in the case of Highlander 2: The Quickening he has saved himself a couple hours of misery and Sean Connery hamming it up.

problem when the question is his mum asking, 'Do you want ketchup on your chips Zed?'. It was truly a cold tea in the Turpin family home that night.

Zed is a lore master and knows many of the laws, rules, guidelines, regulations, precedents, decrees, unwritten agreements and playground rules[16]. He uses these scholarly powers to...well it's not easy to tell, the man is such an enigma he hasn't exactly been pinned down on his aims yet. Still anyone running a quest wants him on their side, because you know, he *looks* like he knows stuff.

Zed is also a member of CAMRA[17] and has been to every Holts pub in the known galaxy and is currently seeking funding for an expedition to see if there are any Holts pubs beyond EGS-zs8-1. Zed has a sneaking suspicion there is, and that the beer will taste exactly the same there.

Zed speaks in what he believes is ye olde English but is more accurately described as ye olde bollockes.

Alex Stackhouse:

The protagonist[18] of our piece, although the most heroic thing they ever did was let an old lady have their seat on the bus. At least they

---

[16] He still struggles with the full rules of Monopoly, often trying to erect campsites on Old Park Lane
[17] Bearded and weird. Of course he is.
[18] Or antagonist, depends on your point of view, I guess.

thought it was an old lady, turned out it was Ronnie Wood from the Rolling Stones.

Alex lives at home with their parents or 'the cheapest hotel in town' as they call it to the amusement of no humans. Though a passing mayfly once heard the line and chuckled a little, not much.

If ever a person was less cut out to save the world its Alex. Their hobbies are sleeping, drinking, eating Pound Bakery pasties (often sharing a causal link with the drinking) and having an encyclopaedic knowledge of the films of Arnold Schwarzenegger (which once got them out of a tight spot with an angry badger, those crazy action movie loving badgers).

Alex was once told by an elaborately dressed elderly lady with beads (so clearly a witch) that they were destined for great things. Alex took this as a sign of their destiny as something important. Alas the lady said 'grate' things, having felt Alex was likely to end up working in a cheese grating factory. Alex is using destiny to sort out their life, as they can't be bothered to do it themselves at the moment.

Alex works in the administration department of their Local Authority. Alex is regularly late, misses deadlines, sends emails to the wrong person, ignores answering the phone, spends a chunk of their day on the internet and fiddles their time sheet. Alex is regarded as a 'valued' member of the Local Authority.

Alex knows one day destiny will take them out of their current life and to a spot on one of the copious not especially funny panel shows that populate TV.

Queen Helena; The a Bit Stern:

On Planet Eccles society is extremely unfairly weighted towards women[19]. Think your average golf members club bar, but with less people wearing chinos *and* pringle sweaters. Due to this Queen Helena can never truly run the planet, by law, even though she de facto does as her husband King Russ of the Abbott is a lazy sod who spends his days playing black hole golf[20], or arranging 'grand openings' of places (pubs usually).

Queen Helena must do all the planet admin including the retails arm of the royal biscuits which retail at the very reasonable price of fifty space bucks, your left kidney and the tear of a wildebeest. Helena is very bitter at all this work she takes on whilst everyone still kowtows to her husband.

Helena would like to be acknowledged as the extreme ruler so she can pay staff exactly the minimum wage, and not a penny more, to do all the administrative tasks. This will free her up to pursue her twin passions of setting up charities

---

[19] Like Earth basically.

[20] An easy game for simpletons. Although most of the game is spent making leery comments about women or members of staff the players work with. Avoid at all costs.

to further women's rights and hunting and skinning small rodents (voles mainly).

Helena is known as 'The Stern', not due especially from any form of fierceness, but as the ~~Ecclesonians,~~ ~~Ecclesees,~~ Ecclestons carry the tradition of naming ships after their queens. Unfortunately, they misunderstood the concept of this naming convention and named the back part of the ship after her. Ever since then this sobriquet has stuck, much to Helena's chagrin. She can be quite stern too.

What Helena needs is something that gives her ultimate power over the universe, although she may have failed to realise with ultimate power comes increased admin and personal appearances at the unveiling of space yachts. Still, she rationalises all this with the fact she has greater motivation than Hollywood bothers to invest in most of its villains.

Helena is essentially benevolent (unless you're a vole) but a bit miffed and highly motivated. And anyone who has met a middle manager that is miffed and highly motivated can attest that's a combination to be feared.

Jane Admin (nee Bigduds):

Jane does Queen Helena's administration. She loves admin, especially form filling, report writing and cost benefit analysis creation. She has been known to ask for excel spreadsheets for Christmas. She is a big fan of the Earthen TV show Call the Midwife.

Jane is exceedingly loyal to Queen Helena and wants her to be happy even though Helena seems to spend most of her time yelling at Jane and failing to comprehend the importance of signing her name within the box on the forms Jane brings her. Essentially it's a standard employer/employee relationship.

Jane is a highly decorated Eccleston war veteran who took part in many intergalactic battles but found the space rapier was not as much fun as the space clipboard, as the expression on Planet Eccles nearly goes.

Chapter 4.5 – Searching for originality in the bargain basement of a poundshop.

Kevin Mung-O-Jerry Mung (Kevin to people who don't like him[21]), paused from the riddle in front of him. Wracking his brains, looking for the solution to this infernal conundrum. No, it was no use, he would have to give up on the soduko puzzle confounding him and return to his work as the master archivist on the planet Expositiongonia.

Picking up the dusty tome from the table in front of him, he turned to the pages on planet and lunar alignment. Suddenly something hit him, his heart lurched, something was wrong, badly wrong, what was in front of him made no sense. Realising this was as he hadn't put his glasses on yet he calmed down before returning to the page in the book.

Looking at the ledger in front of him, his heart dropped again, that was it he was giving up the Pallian Vindaloo eggs. Still, dodgy diet aside, the page made for grim reading, he took the words in and blew his cheeks out in tension. He strode to the bookcase and looked up all the words he didn't understand (which was most of them, though he remembered 'orbit' was something to do with chewing gum).

No, by his rough calculations, the page revealed a terrible truth, and he would need to raise the alarm, he did a half-hearted re-

---

[21] Kevin to pretty much everyone then.

calculation to confirm his fears and his calculation looked like it may be about right, give or take.

The archivist would have to let the high chamberlain know as a matter of extreme urgency. He took off his glasses and neatly folder the dust cloth around them before placing them back in their case, he orderly placed his suduko book back on the shelf and checked the tv guide to see if there was anything to watch later. Satisfied it was all repeats he ambled to the door.

Kevin pulled open the large chamber doors. He strolled (with an occasional strut thrown in to beat the boredom) down the checked floor patterned hallway, passing the badly crayoned art on the walls of previous high Chamberlains and Master Archivists[22].

Reaching the lift, he pressed the button for the Freddie Star chamber. Ascending 200 floors he realised it was floor 8 he needed and pressed the correct button. 120 minutes later[23] he reached the correct floor, a little bored and regretting not going to the toilet before he left his chamber.

Exiting the lift, Kevin strode down leopard skin lined corridors[24] reaching the security gate.

---

[22] Expositiongonia art is an acquired taste, in the same way the scent of a chemical toilet is an acquired smell.

[23] Expositiongonia measure everything in minutes, except Roger Bannister's 4-minute mile which they call the '0.15th of an hour mile'. Don't ask me why.

[24] again, taste isn't the Exposition onia's strong suit.

"This is a highly restricted area, what is your purpose?" demanded the burly security guard, putting down his copy of a Barbara Cartland novel.

"I must see the high Chamberlain as a matter of extreme urgency!" demanded Kevin.

"OK." The guard said stepping aside and offering a flourish as he pointed in the direction of the large elaborate door at the end of the corridor.

"What?! Don't you want to see my credentials?" Kevin (fairly reasonably)
asked.

"Nah. You've got an honest face" replied the security guard "Plus I saw a blue crayon picture that looked just like you in the corridor. Well, I say it looked like you, I had to close one eye, squint a bit and hop on one leg, but no mistaking those noble features. I passed it when I went to the toilet earlier, if you ask me, it's a very long way to go for a tinkle, and surely, I should have another guard with me as it gets very lonely guarding this gate, no one uses it anyway. Did you see Weststarters[25] last night? Totally unrealistic, as if Granite would sleep with Shamrock, I mean…"

The words echoed hollowly down the empty corridor, as Kevin had long since breezed past with something of a flounce.

---

[25] A popular but tedious soap opera on the planet.

Kevin waddled through the main door and came to some patio doors which he burst through urgently, before going back to make sure they were shut properly. He wound his way around a maze of pot plants and plot pants before entering through a hidden side door bringing him in a large room that was next door to the chamber Kevin had made his discovery in[26].

Entering the chamber, he approached the throne of the high chamberlain. "Master, I have news of utmost urgency, it concerns a pointless planet, many solar systems from here. There is a terrible item that if it falls into the wrong hands at the wrong time then the universe could immediately be sent into dominion with…"

"…Stuart."

"What?!" spluttered the archivist.

"Don't call me master, it makes me feel old. Call me Stuart." The High Chamberlain had been on an improving employee relations course and was told everyone calling each other by first names would improve work morale. It wouldn't.

"OK Stuart, it concerns the planet Earth. The co-ordinates to the rubber glove of ultimate power (and reasonable water proofing) have been revealed somehow and we are reaching the required full moon in seven days on the

---

[26] Expositiongonia building planning is notoriously ropey

planet where it has lay hidden and if the glove is under the moonbeam on the anointed slot and the allotted time, then its full awesome power will be activated".

The high chamberlain flinched slightly as the utter cliché being explained to him unfolded but went with it as the archivist had sold it to him with gusto.

"You know they have full moons pretty regularly on Earth? The ancient philosopher Patrick of Moore taught us thus".

"Yes, I know, but this one is different for some hokum, as all the scriptures point to this being the moon that will power the glove that can rule the universe. And somehow the closely guarded secrets if its whereabouts have become known." Kevin tailed off when explaining the last sentence, not entirely convinced in the plausibility of what he was selling.

"Hmmm. OK let me see." Mused the High Chamberlain. He rose from his throne (more of an elaborate chair with a little gilding truth be told) and shuffled to his enormous four storey bookcase (this was a problem for the people on the two floors above who had their space seriously compromised. Less so for those three floors above as this was a toilet floor and the books offered 'contingency' to those lacking toilet paper. The high chamberlain was regularly perplexed by the missing pages when doing his research through books from the high shelf).

"Now where do I start?" he scanned the ancient volumes that held the secrets of many galaxies (and a couple of Mars bars) his hand traced along the books muttering to himself, 'Understanding the Universe for dummies', 'Gloves with the power to rule the entire universe', 'How to sound like you know a lot about the galaxy to impress women at parties'" before resting "ah here it is", the chamberlain pulled the laptop from the bookshelf. He returned to his throne.

"Have you seen my glasses?"

"They're on your head Stuart" The archivist returned neutrally.

"So they are." The high chamberlain turned and saw his glasses perched on
the head of his stuffed former headmaster[27].

The high chamberlain began to key in some letters, his eyes suddenly widening "Curses! Damn you to hell!!" he screamed, face puce with rage "I'll install the bloody anti-virus software later!". After a pause he looked at the master archivist, "I'm not finding it".

"How are you spelling it...mas...maStuart?" The Archivist asked.

---

[27] Exposiongonia customs dictate that those that reach the role of high chamberlain will have their former school headmaster stuffed and placed in their chamber. It's a high honour.

"E-R-F?" The High Chamberlain stated back his voice lacking any conviction.

"No, it's earth, sod."

"I beg your padawan?!" It was Kevin's turn to flinch as the last word brought back painful memories of The Phantom Menace.

"No sod, as in the space soil in the palace gardens." The archivist clarified.

"Everything has 'space' as a prefix around here…" muttered the High Chamberlain. "Wait, oh yes got it, it's the planet that gave us Pringles right?"

"That's the one"

"So, let me get this right" began the high chamberlain in hushed tones "There is a glove of extreme power hidden on planet Earth, which has had its existence revealed somehow and in seven days' time a special moon will rise and give the wearer the power to shape the universe to their destiny if stood in the anointed spot. And given that all races and species will be aware of this fact, and let's face it there are a lot of rum 'uns out there, this power could fall into the hands of evil, if a hero doesn't prevail and find it first. And ting?"

That sums up the entire plot, I mean danger, very explicitly Stuart." The archivist confirmed grimly. A long, long, loooonnngggg (it's really rather long) pause enveloped the two.

"Is that it?" The High Chamberlain asked.

"What do you mean Stuart?"

"What do we do now, Master Archivist?"

"Nothing Stuart. Our role is to set up the plot, I mean see the danger, and then we're not in the story, I mean involved in doing anything about this danger again."

"Bugger that! I want more scenes, I mean involvement! Prepare the pan planetary canoe, we have work to do." The High Chamberlain ordered.

The archivist bowed. The chamberlain hadn't removed that piece of subsiquis….subseek…susequies…that bit of bottom kissing. He now had a choice; spend eight hours going back to his chambers for the anti-chaffing cream for the canoe journey, or take the seventeen hours journey the other way to start up the canoe. It was going to be a long week and if he wasn't lucky in 28 days, 31 tops, it would be a long month.

Chapter the first – keep me hanging on the throne

Queen Helena eased herself onto the imposing gilt-edged throne[28]. She wasn't in the best mood, which put her mood somewhere around that of a 14-year-old girl with a confiscated phone and a Hippo that was having root canal surgery by an amateur baboon[29]. She had been planning a day of drinking Nurgling gin[30] and racing her hyper-chariot around the nearest quasar, but instead had been called to court for some vital administrative work. Administrator Prime Jane Bigduds (nee Admin) tentatively stepped up to the throne.

"Apologies majesty, but these warrants need royal approval as a matter of urgency" Jane spoke timidly, trying to avoid looking Helena in the eye.

"And my husband?" Helena asked archly, staring Jane up and down and left and right to make sure she had all the main angles covered.

"He has vital royal business…"

"…pissed up on a golf course" Helena cut Jane off with a shake of her head. "Very well, what do we have?"

---

[28] From the Strongman range in Ikea. Only four light years from the exit once entered. The meat balls are average.

[29] Professional baboons are available if you have the funds.

[30] Guaranteed to have you waking up crying in a flowerbed or your money back.

"This first warrant is what colour to paint the walls of the royal toilet, purple, mauve or magenta." Jane began eagerly. She pulled out a colour chart and unspooled it, the paper cascading across the polished marble of the throne room floor.

"This, this is what you interrupted my gin...never mind, what's the point, let's go mauve" Helena said, heart not in the discussion. Not in the room.

"Excellent choice Highness which shade of mauve? Do you want 'guts of a suckling pig' mauve or 'I see dead people' mauve?" Jane caught Helena's fierce look and quickly moved on "Mauve mauve it is, an excellent choice. Next we need a decision on what you think the threat level is of the Grotlings from the planet TotesToasties is" Jane asked, getting into a confident rhythm now that she was in the thick of admin, which she truly loved.

"How likely is it?" Helena asked trying her best to engage.

"We're not sure. Detailed military intelligence rates its chances of happening as 'possibly'." Jane concluded.

"And the colour rating options?" Helena asked staring distractedly out of the high arched window at the majesty of the green Eccles sun rising. It was a good Chinese Take away.

"There is a colour chart for this too" Jane began eagerly reaching for a large parchment in her knapsack.

"Red. Red will do", Helena said with a dismissive wave of her hand and a very dismissive wave of her earlobe.

Helena turned her mourning gaze from the sun and the possibilities of the outdoors to Jane, Jane visibly shrunk, an impressive feat as she was only 2 foot 6 to start with. "Any other Business Administrator Prime?"

"We call it AOB" Jane beamed back.

"Which means?" Helena beamed, probably to some other planet where you could drink Nurgling gin.

"Any Other Business!" Jane declared happily

"Oh for f…" Helena was thinking it was going to take diesel cut Black Lace Agadoo vodka to wash away the tedium of this day. "Any, I mean AOB?"

Jane checked her data slate muttering to herself "Potential black hole consuming Eccles…no that can wait until we've had the risk assessment, possible sequel to Jaws the Revenge, no that's not for Royal Approval yet, should cats be allowed in the cinema if accompanied by a responsible adult, do fire extinguishers need to have 'use only in the event of a fire' warning stickers on them? Should people taking full trolleys to the self-service checkout be exterminated, not that's a pet project…oh there is one thing." Jane put the data slate back in its case and produced another long parchment and unfurled it, the end rolled out of the throne room and the distant sound of "Oi watch it!" could be heard echoing back from the corridor.

Helena slumped further in her throne and scowled at Jane.

"Well your Majestical one, researchers have discovered a glove that when charged gives the wearer ultimate power over the universe…" Jane looked up and saw an expression on Helena's face she couldn't place, she assumed it was trapped wind "…we can look at that another time".

"Wait!" Helena bellowed her voice reverberating around the chamber. A courtier who had misheard came running in with a dumbbell, realised their mistake and ran out again.

Jane heard the sound of a penny dropping "Sorry!" called the guard fumbling with his change by the snack machine.

"You've just got my undivided attention" Helena declared, leaning forward a smirk playing across her lips. Hopscotch probably.

"Oh, the glove thingy?" Jane regarded Helena "Yes we can definitely look into that."

Chapter Next - Magical Mystery Bore

Somewhere[31] on IzzyWhizzyLetsGetBusyDonia[32], Suzie entered the hut of the Elder[33]. The Elder sat cross legged on a multi-coloured Ikea rug whilst potions bubbled away on unevenly built shelves in the background. Rumour had it the elder was trying to synthesise an affordable fruit smoothie, but most felt that was witchcraft beyond even her considerable means.

The Elder put down her Ladybird book of magical geese on the floor and motioned for Suzie to join her on the rug, Suzie wondered why they couldn't sit on the comfy sofa in the corner of the hut, but complied with the request. The elder offered Suzie a cup, Suzie took a draught, a steaming bubbling dreamlike liquid assaulted her senses "Ah warm fizzy Vimto," she declared satisfied.

"Thank you for coming Suzie", the Elder began her voice cracked and croaky, probably from having the air condition on in the hut too long. "We have noted your progress with a very watchful eye, of course we keep the other watchful eye on the bingo numbers – it's got to be our turn soon right?" The elder seemed to drift away on her thoughts, then came back to herself "Kudos on defeating the Fleetwood-Mac

---

[31] Almost certainly Suzie's village all things considered.

[32] Sign writers on the planet have be known to suffer Carpal Tunnel Syndrome.

[33] A name disliked by the Elder, who is only 46, but that's tradition for you.

dragon of Middleoftheroadonia. We now believe you have honed your craft to make yourself the most powerful wizard of our number.

"Oh thanks." Suzie blushed, "It was nothing really, I got a bit lucky with some of the spells", she deflected modestly "I really didn't think the giant marriage guidance counsellor I conjured was going to be so effective".

"The timing of you reaching this status is very fortuitous, almost a complete fluke that makes no sense if you take time to ponder it. But let's not do that." The Elder seemed to speed up her talking "There is serious stuff afoot. Possibly as high as the knee" The Elder stated, Suzie leaned forward looking her in her non-Bingo eye, when they clashed noses, she realised she had leaned too far. "There is news of discovery, a troubling discovery. What those that came before me called 'The Marigold of Bossiness'[34], has had its whereabouts revealed."

"And were this to fall in the wrong hands, or in this case hand, the whole world would potentially be subjected to tyranny and oppression?" Suzie enquired.

The Elder caught her breath, "Blimey! I didn't realise you had mastered the power of reading the nylon strings of the future as well. Well I don't need to tell you the need" The Elder

---

[34] IzzyWhizzyLetsGetBusyDonians struggle with suitably dramatic names

began, before going on to tell her the need "that given the severity of this situation, I want you to quest to retrieve the glove so that no evil may have it. Make this the highest priority you have. Actually finish making the balloons shaped like animals for my daughter's birthday party first yeah?"

Suzie smiled and nodded. Walruses. She most liked making the walruses.

"Also", the Elder sat upright, "the elder, elders, the elderests, also foresaw a prophecy. A being of such great power, or something, that may tame the powers of the glove and lead the universe in a direction of peace and prosperity, or at the very least a period of 'meh-ness'. See if you can look them up while you're out please?" The Elders words dripped portent, mostly as she had yet to book in a portent plumber to fix that.

Suzie rubbed her hands together in satisfaction, a gesture that no one does anymore. "Sounds like a laugh, count me in" she chuckled, and rose to her feet gingerly, trying to regain the feeling in her legs, buttocks and her right tricep. She bowed and made her way to the hut door.

"Suzie" The Elder called after her "Be careful, we're talking about the fate of the universe here". Her words heavy and ominous.

Suzie nodded solemnly, "Yeah I'll give it a whirl. These things usually work out OK". Suzie grabbed the handle of the hut door, turned and pulled. After a few seconds she pushed instead "why would you have a handle facing in on a push door…?" she muttered to herself but speaking for the galaxy.

"Suzie" The Elder called again, a tremor in her powerful voice, Suzie turned and faced back "Can you put the bin out on your way to the gate please?"

Suzie left the hut and picked up the black bin which rattled heavily to the sound of glass bottles and cans, she played the news she had just heard around in her head. The prophecies had always warned there would be a point where the universe would be tested and the forces of light and dark would collide and she, Suzie, Master of the Wizards was going to get a mention in the credits. She rolled the bin and left it unevenly by the gate, wandering off whistling a bright but tuneless ditty to herself.

"Green bin this week!" a muffled voice bellowed from inside the hut.

Chapter here – Beard and loafing in a duck pond

Sara the witch, who's moniker came from her liking for dying her hair purple, wearing a Nine Inch Nails hoodie and owning a black cat and because, well some people are really unimaginative with nicknames and Eva the not a witch, who got her name as she is different from Sara and some people are really binary with nicknames, waded through the green pond water and clambered into the floating mystical tent of Kazoomie[35]. "Zed you called for us using the ancient smoke signal?" Sara spoke to the robed figure splayed comfortably out on the tent floor.

"Drat! I musteth learnedly to have a crafty pipeth smoke more craftilyeth...I mean actually yes I did send for thee!" Zed smiled broadly at the pair, though the effect was lost in the confines of his beard. He straightened up, which was more of an inelegant slouch truth be told.

"This must be a matter of great import" Eva spoke as she lowered herself into sitting cross legged on the canvas across from Zed "Why do you need us?"

Surprisingly lithely, Zed sprung up, smacked his head on the canvas and adopted a crouch. "Well thy called the deux of thee to ensure this wasn't a doubleheader dynamic again" Sara

---

[35] Part of Millets 'Enigma statement' range, a real talking point at any festival or campsite.

and Eva exchanged puzzled looks but remained silent. "I verily must set offeth on a quest to find the mystival glove of power as mentioned in the footnotes of the scriptures[36], it's close to reaching its ripening of powerery".

Sara stiffened a shudder went down her spine, but that may have been the lack of central heating in the tent "then the stories of this glove are more than fables from the mists of time?"

"Quack" said a stray duck that had stuck its head in the cramped tent.

"Verily it is real." Zed confirmed fixing both the ladies in the eye, which was disconcerting as they were sat behind each other in the tent. "And I will use all my mystic powers to preventedly evil having its way." Zed continued "Also the appendix of the scriptures mentioneth some person who perchance can take the powers of thy glove and use them correctdly, so I'll see if can meet cute with thee."

Zed turned behind him to an elaborate dressing table at the back of the tent, "Now let's celebrate this missions conception, I've createdeth this nouveau home brew and thy would loveth to share with thee! Plus, I thought now would be a good time to discuss which was the besteth Radioheadeth album over a pint of it."

Zed reached over to the dresser and picked up an elaborate crystal cut decanter. He popped

---

[36] It really is – see!

the top off, with smoke bubbling from the brew beneath. He proceeded to pour the liquid into three finely carved plastic travel beakers and offered two cups to his companions who were making themselves as comfortable as possible on the ground sheet, as anyone who has laid across a groundsheet knows this is about as comfortable as sleeping on a vibrating bed of nails whilst there is rumour of a hungry alligator somewhere in your house.

"Well it has to be The Bends" Eva ventured, "its raw emotional angst set to perfect minor key melody." Eva took a large swig from the cup, the liquid tasted surprisingly, but not unpleasantly of Primula chive flavour. The burning of all her nasal hair was more of a concern.

Sara cocked her head and considered what Eva had said. "Too teenage angst", she concluded. "Sure the melodies are beautiful, but the lyrics? I give you In Rainbows for your consideration. It brings the melodies but marries them with unpredictable beats and more unexpected structures." Sara drew on her brew, for some reason it tasted of green Skittles, she felt her brain do a quick lap of her cranium before setting itself back in its natural place, hopefully facing the right way and still fully plumbed in.

Zed stroked his beard. Five minutes later he spoke, "both verily fine choices he concluded sagely (with a bit of onionly) "but for thee it has to be Kid A."

"Why is that?" Eva asked leaning on her elbow falling off her elbow then giving up on any attempted elbow balancing.

"As I like to get wastedly in a field and dance like a madmanly to banging beats!" Zed declared triumphantly managing a little jig on his hunched spot.

"Quack" agreed the duck.

At this point all three and the duck (who had inhaled enough brew fumes to floor a concrete reinforced rhino) collapsed into a heap of drunken slumber on the tent floor. Zed's mission would be delayed by a few days and a couple of fry ups. This was not an unusual state of affairs for the great mystic before he partook in a quest.

Here is a Chapter – Meet your new hero, same as the old hero, well pretty similar in most respects

Alex stirred from their deep slumber. An age-old truism dawning on their very being, as the answer echoed back to the conundrum from the eternities "Arse I'm gonna be late for work!" Alex yelped, whilst letting out a loud early morning surprise fart.

After an extremely long and not entirely enjoyable wee, Alex hurriedly threw on some clothes that lay scattered around their bedroom floor, some of which were even done up correctly and on the right parts of their body. The enigma of finding the missing odd sock would have to wait for later when Alex could call in reinforcements for the search party. Using a combination of running, stumbling and falling, Alex made it downstairs to the kitchen.

"Afternoon!" teased Alex's dad, using a joke Alex must have heard nearly every week of their life. Maybe not getting up late would prevent the opportunity for this razor-sharp piece of wit. Though that seemed too much like effort to Alex, so they would endure these dull barbs yet.

"Lively night?" asked Alex's mum "you may want to brush your teeth as you smell like a brewers' underpants. And not his good clean pants at that either". Alex's head told them the truth of the statement, it felt like the hamster had taken some time off the wheel to do some head renovation using the modern decorating tools of a jack hammer and TNT.

"I just had a quick pint after work with the team." Alex stated. "It was Kate's leaving do or Amy's. I think. I'm a little hazy as one of the two pints was clearly a little off." Alex picked up some bread toying with the idea of making a packed lunch before their dad handed them a bag of already made lunch. Alex nodded their appreciation and regretted it as the hamster seemed to take up pogo sticking in a lead diving suit. "I wasn't going to go out, but I couldn't have Emily leave without having a few quick halves with them. I'll miss Hannah, I really will, but its nice I got to have three pints with her".

Alex's mum raised an eyebrow, then released in into the wild. "I'll give you a lift to work on my way in, but you have five minutes.". .

"Breakfast first!" Alex's dad declared triumphantly plonking a mass of yellow, brown, off white, cream and beige slop on a plate for Alex.

"Jackson Pollock Breakfast. Great!" Alex declared to themselves. Alex took a bite of something brown and vaguely sausage shaped, thinking it was the foulest tasting thing in the universe. Clearly Alex wasn't aware of Fresno Bob the celebrity chef from the planet Gastroenteritis and his famous Gort anus sausage and prune blancmange dish.

"Hey, that's a cordon bleu dish!" came a voice from the planet Gastroenteritis as an indignant Fresno Bob regretted his phsychic powers to hear the thoughts of anyone thinking about his dishes, regardless of where on the universe they were having these food based thoughts.

Alex finished the breakfast in record time wondering which had done more damage, eating a piping hot breakfast and damaging the roof of their mouth, or just eating their dad's breakfast full stop. Why Alex's dad put a full stop in his breakfasts, Alex couldn't work out.

Alex battled to get their hands through the sleeves of their coat, a task that seemingly went from the straightforward to Knightmare[37] difficulty based on the alcohol the night before ratio. "Lisa not getting a lift?"

"Your little sister was up an hour ago and left for work before any of us were up." Alex's dad responded, "I need to check the milkman from 22 years ago didn't have a particularly strong work ethic.". Alex heard his mum snort a laugh and smiled to themself. The only challenge remained for Alex was working out why one shoe was in the hallway and the other in the upstairs toilet.

****

Alex's mum was driving particularly aggressively this morning. She seemed to be

---

[37] And with no Treguard to assist when Alex asked, "Where am I?".

trying to amuse herself with a game of 'near touchy bumper' with any car that had the misfortune of pulling in front of her. "What have you got on at work today?" she enquired.

"Err…I'm not sure really, I think I have to…err…empty the trash bin on my desktop. That'll take a few hours. But tonight, I'm going to dust down my CV and start applying for some jobs, it's about time I put my philosophy degree to work in my career. Oh, and in my weekends, I'm going to start developing that book I'm working on.". Said book, was a notepad with 'insert title' here written in big letters on the first page and not much else. Well, nothing else.

"How many chapters are you in now?" Alex's mum asked.

"Well you see, the thing is…uh…I don't really like to work off chapters, its more free form, stream of conscious like Ulysses (Alex pretended they knew something about the book). And I've got some great character synopsis in my head."

"Look Alex…For Cripes sake what the bloody hell was that!!" Alex's mum's voice went from soothing to raging monster at the speed of a Conservative Peer moving from room to room after being told there is a pretty girl in a short skirt somewhere in the hotel they are staying in. "Alex, any person who has friends can't be considered a failure. All we want for you is that you're happy and friends will always give you that, whether you're counting paperclips or running the planet. You're as successful as we ever wanted. So, if you take anything from this journey its I'M GOING TO STICK THAT WINDSCREEN WIPER UP YOUR ARSE! HAVE YOU NOT HEARD OF INDICATING[38]?!" Alex's mum bellowed face pressed to the windscreen to add extra 'umph' to her threat.

"It's OK mum, I can walk from here." Alex said in a voice register so high the Bee Gee's would have rejected it as making a mockery of their songs. Alex found themselves attempting exiting the car whilst it was still moving. Alex's mum brought the car to an aggressive stop "And mum thanks for… just thanks." Alex planted a kiss on her cheek and left sharply.

---

[38] And if the person is in an Audi, the answer to that question is 'no'. Ditto to the questions 'have you heard of acknowledging when someone lets you through?' and 'Have you ever tried not tailgating?'.

Chapter On! Clocking in (more than a little earlier than the actual time you reached the building) Tuning Out and Logging Off

"Alex, you're late even by your standards. In fact, by the time that computer takes to boot up[39] the sun will have burnt out leaving the planet as a dying husk!" Claire mock admonished Alex as they attempted a crouch slide into their office chair, as if that would make it look like they had been sat there all along.

"Mother bloody Theresa speaks!" Alex flashed back with a grin. "Has Genghis noticed I'm late?" Alex asked nervously eying up and down the banks of open plan desks.

"Hard to tell." Claire mused "Your being late is kind of taken as a given. That she hasn't said anything to you is a worry, I think she is planning something. Be afraid. Very afraid. What's the excuse this time?" Claire' words came out in more of a stream of conscious "Abducted by aliens and probed, but then left alone when they found nothing of substance?".

"Something like that. I threw a Gregg's steak pasty at them and the confusing piece of matter was beyond their comprehension and they fled!" Alex repeatedly hammered on the space bar trying to get their monitor out of sleep mode, clearly the monitor felt like Alex.

---

[39] Public sector computers start up times are measure in ice ages

Claire nodded, "You know it's your Personal Development Meeting[40] today?" she said with the smirk of someone knowing they were supplying news the other person wouldn't want to hear.

"Oh, bugger yeah!" Alex cursed "one minute.", Alex quickly opened up their write up from the previous year and hit 'ctrl and C', then 'Ctrl and V' on a newly opened Word document. "et voila, what do you think?" they asked Claire.

Claire leaned across, Alex enjoyed picking up the pleasant scent of an above average price perfume from Boots in their nostrils. "You need to change the date to this year. Oh, and maybe take my name off it this time, yeah?" Claire threw her head back and let out her dirty laugh. "Now make me a brew, it's a job even you can do. Remember it tastes better when you actually boil the kettle."

At this point a slimy, tentacled alien with rotating eyes teleported into the centre of the office "Surprise! Space! Science Fiction! Anyone...Anyone?!" Scanning the cluttered office (which is pretty easy with rotating eyes) the alien saw that everyone was more intent on

---

[40] For those that have never had a Personal Development meeting, it's like a game of call my bluff. You completely exaggerate your achievements, or take credit for someone else's work, your line manager takes this all as fact as they can't remember what you've done as they have too much work on to bother worrying about your achievements. You then agree targets for next year that neither will do anything about. Repeat and rinse.

staring blankly at their screens, sneakily trying to send personal emails to mates similarly bored two desks down, or sneakily using their phone to send a message to someone two desks down. "Sod this!" said Kenneth[41] and teleported off to see if he could get a bet on the 14:22 from Cheltenham, a slug beast in a bar had told him there was a horse in the field that was a dead cert[42].

****

Five cups of strong tea (relying on 'borrowing' milk from co-worker's clearly labelled bottles[43]) and Alex was in the zone at work. Unfortunately, that 'zone' was a parents and children parking area in some black hole on some far away galaxy, but it was still a zone.

Watching Salma pass his desk, Alex spotted a chance "Salma, will you help me with my appraisal? Make it all decent and that?"

"And after that can you turn the contents of the water cooler into wine?" Claire piped up. Crack piped up maybe. Alex shot Claire a look that was aiming for stern consternation but came

---

[41] Popular name on the planet Demolition Man

[42] Said horse came last by 70 furlongs but was also disqualified for attempting to tap dance (not easy in horseshoes) its way around the course. Which just proves the old adage that you should never trust the tip of a giant slug beast in bar.

[43] Hopefully avoiding the one someone put the laxative in as an 'anti-theft deterrent'. Though as tactics go it does render the milk unusable for the owner, unless they enjoy brapping their pants.

across as something between confused and constipated.

Salma was Alex's Assistant Team Leader and was the soft kind hand hidden in the steel glove. Unlike Alex's actual Team Leader, Jamie, who was a bony fist clenching a knuckleduster in a spiked rusty metal gauntlet.

"Sure." Salma concluded and took the empty chair next to Alex. "Let's role play it[44]." Alex looked around desperately at his desk for anything that might end their life and spare this humiliation. Reasoning the stapler (literally) wouldn't cut it, Alex nodded. "So, you're late to your appraisal Alex, why is that?"

"Wait a minute, why are you saying I'm late?!" Alex asked affronted.

"You will be." Smirked Salma, Claire made no attempt to suppress her mirth across the desk.

"I was stuck on the toilet as I have the squits?!" Alex asked tentatively. There was some truth in this, being on large quantities of lager with a soupcon of a late-night kebab last night, Alex's insides were as delicate as a damp toilet paper doilee being used to carry dinosaur eggs.

"Well if that's the excuse you're going for, sure, why not." Salma stared Alex in the eye "What is your biggest achievement this year? Besides

---

[44] There are two terrifying things in this universe, the horror beasts from the planet Waarrgghh!! And work-based role plays.

being in on time that day Jamie offered to buy us all breakfast?".

"Well I...I...I checked all the reports on the Excel spreadsheet and totalled the value" Alex stated a sense of pride kicking in.

"Those that were listed on the spreadsheet already? So, you pressed autosum on column G?" Salma asked her stare not breaking an inch from where Alex was starting to perspire, as beer sweated out of their system.

"Err, yeah. I put them in alphabetical order too."

"So, you know the sort button too. Good work. But you did complete the returns for the adhoc accounts?" Salma probed.

"Actually, no I didn't" Alex focused their attention on watching the fan on the desk spinning around, it was almost hypnotic.

Salma smiled "It doesn't matter Alex, just say you did. Management in here entirely assess us on the monthly report and as long as the boxes show green on that, they're happy. They don't actually know what you do, so tell them what they want to hear, and they'll be happy."

Salma stood up and Alex relaxed a little "though stop walking around the office with that clipboard trying to look purposeful, everyone does that when they're first attempting to master the trying to look busy look. You'll be fine Alex, you're a decent member of the team. Spelling your name correctly passes as an achievement for some in here." And with that,

Salma picked up a clipboard off the desk and strode off with a flourish.

****

Inside one of the numerous dull offices, Jamie sat at a desk, distracted by the noise of construction work going on over the road to build the new G4S office which was taking over most public sector work which had been subcontracted out to them due to the owners of the company having the important qualification of having been to the same private school as the person awarding the contract. Alex rushed through the door "Sorry I'm late Jaime, I have the squi...never mind, sorry."

After this the dull dance of banal pleasantries the appraisal hit full swing with meaningess platitudes, over exaggerated claims of success, business expressions no one fully understood the meaning of and unearned thank yous were batted around.

"You did a good job collating the returns for the adhoc account Alex, I was very impressed with that" Jamie said reading from Alex's write up. "Can I speak openly Alex?" Alex felt their stomach lurch and this probably wasn't the lager/kebab combo. "You're a good worker and..." at this point the G4S sign on the crane over the road spun round so that the four blocked the windowpane casting shade on Alex. "that's a big four shadow." Jamie remarked with a grimace "Alex you have the potential to be what you want, where you go is in your hands, you can achieve incredible things." The crane moved the four away from the window. "Who knows. In five to ten years you could be the deputy senior office administrator. You just need to focus and apply yourself to achieve anything. So, I've agreed you will action[45] fifty calculations a day or you'll get a written warning." And with that Jamie shuffled the papers in front of them "So that's agreed."

"Thanks Jamie." Alex declared neutrally and picked up their notes in front of them (written in the biggest font which still looked realistic and not what it really was - an attempt to take up page space to seem like they had done lots of things in the year) and strode of to brag in the canteen about their potential.

---

[45] 'Action', or as it's known outside business bollocks speak; 'do'.

Chapter: The Herman and Hit

Luci made her way to her father's caravan on the park in Fleetwood. The rain seemed to hit her face from above and below with a little from the side thrown in for good measure and the slate grey sky spread in all directions rendering visibility to about the distance posh people need to use their car to get the shops. Luci mused on how it was such an unexpectedly nice day in these parts.

Opening the Space Crusading Ox[46] door Luci stepped into the oppressive gloom, this was truly a caravan like any other. In the centre of the kitchen worktop lay a piece of paper glowing as if illuminated by the gods. With practiced trepidation, Luci approached cautiously. On closer inspection, a torch had been unconvincingly cellotaped above it as a makeshift spotlight. Luci picked up the note:

'My darling daughter, by miracle you found my letter...'

"And it was so cunningly hidden too..." muttered Luci. Her dad, the high lord assassin (Ken to the indoor bowling team) would not have appreciated the sarcasm, he was a very literal man, you generally have to be in the

---

[46] Have you ever seen a caravan which doesn't have an oxymoronic name? Next time you're on the motorway relieve the boredom by spotting the caravan with the least fitting name.

assassinating world where nuance is at best discouraged[47].

'I must leave you a quest of great import. I would have taken the quest myself, but we're out of Findus crispy pancakes, and there is a really good episode of Diagnosis murder on later, that Dick Van Dyke, is there anything he can't do? Oh yeah, the accent thing. And his son too, a chip off the old block and in that show on merit I'll wager. Anyway, basically there is this powerful glove thingy, gives the wearer great power, could lead to the universe being enslaved, might be a human who can wield the glove and protect the entire universe etc. etc. The usual really.

So, it's incumbent on you to ensure this item falls into the right hands (pun sort of intended). It's ~~imperative~~…~~impearativ~~…vital you keep this glove away from evil doers. I've put a Post It note on the Universe Atlas to show where you must travel to (as I can't be bothered trying to write directions here). There is five space bucks bus fare in the kitty if you can find him, I'm guessing he's sleeping on one of my freshly pressed shirts somewhere, the bugger. Or maybe chasing a plastic bag down the dual carriageway. Stupid bundle of fur. Oh, and also next to this letter…'

---

[47] Ask Keith the Axe, who when his wife said haphazardly, I'll kill that noisy binman, Keith hunted down the binman and murdered him with a shovel (his nickname proving to be inaccurate at best).

Luci picked up a box on the counter to the left of the letter.

'No, the item to the right.' Continued the letter. Luci sighed and picked up the second box with 'the box' written on a Post It note stuck to it. *'This is one of the most powerful artefacts of our clan'*.

Luci pulled off the elaborate pink ribbon and opened the box pulling out a cream shading to red horn made of some kind of seashell in the shape of a miniature saxophone (alto). Luci turned her attention back to the letter *"You could have waited until I said open the box"* continued the letter. Luci flushed; the toilet was smelling out the caravan. *"This is the Horn of 'Bob Holness Blockbusters'. It is an ancient and powerful item. Blow it at the time of your direst needs and an indestructible army will be summoned. Don't try and play Baker Street on it as the army are sick of hearing it. Use wisely. Certainly, wiser than the great club of Neverwhere I gave you. Honestly that was not for playing crazy golf with. Anyway, I wish you all the luck in the world on your quest, my precious, precious daughter. Love dad".* Luci turned the letter *"PS if you want anything from the shops ring me on my mobile, not the house phone. Hang on, I could have just rung you to relay this message. Bugger it, I've written this much so far, the letter stands. PPS The Iceland has the most amazing range of cheeses in a tube. I know what you're thinking, how did he write about what the shops had in them before he got there? Magic!"*

"Internet shopping." Smiled Luci. "love you daddy". Luci picked up the horn and nimbly twirled it around her fingers before sliding it into her assassin's satchel (containing a variety of pointy things, a sausage role and a thermos of Horlicks). Time to find Mr Didymus, she was going to need the fare for the space train and inevitable intergalactic Megabus replacement service.

Chapter 6: Mutiny with the Bounty Hunter

Barry strode onto his ships command centre, 'The Flying Gerbil' and sat in the nav com chair. Realising this was actually the barber's chair he'd had installed for long hyperspace journey's where his hair started to reach that annoying length you can't do anything with, as casually as he could, he rose quickly to his feet and ambled to the captain's chair.

Taking a minute to weigh up this was the chair he wanted (even though he had written 'Kaptins chare' on it in biro to help his geography) and that Dennis Bergkamp[48] wasn't sat on the bench behind, he sat down. "Ee Zule, this is it, T'big score![49] We rescue some ruddy marigold and we get it to that queen Helena bird, then we get paid enough for us to afford that log cabin in Ilkely we always wanted. I know how much you want to do that, cos I keep telling you how much I want to do that." Barry put his hands behind his head and leant back, now confident that he was sat in the right place.

Zule, who looked as close to a Wookie (crossed with a Datsun Cherry) as is possible without receiving legal papers from Disney and George Lucas[50] looked at Barry from across the command cockpit "Waraharagharagh

---

[48] As happened to the famed space pirate and racist Big Ron of Atkinson 5.

[49] Barry spoke in a regional dialect of Yorkshire known as 'complete stereotype'.

[50] And man, they love their legal papers.

waaaagghhh waraagh!" she roared, then caught herself "sorry I've just sat on my keys." She said in the soothing voice of a Radio 4 presenter. "Great news Barry, how do we do this?"

"As I say, we just pick up this ruddy rubber glove from planet Earth, give it to little miss bossy knickers and we've hit T'Jackpot!". Zule nodded sagely, still not having a clue what Barry was talking about. "Earth, my home town. It'll be bloody brilliant!". Barry's face froze in a warm nostalgic grin, his prominent chin virtually pointing to the woodchip lined cabin ceiling.

Zule was paying particular attention to a bit of dirt under her nails "Oh, er, what are the co-ordinates?" she asked somewhat pertinently.

"Err...lemme see now...err...if you head towards Nebula 4 on the M545541251 bypass and take a second left at T' planet Woodbine then it's just over a couple of roundabouts, watch out for the average speed cameras on Orion's belt." Barry pulled his cap down over his eyes and slouched further into his chair in a gesture of 'I've done my bit'.

Zule blanched, smiled and then just randomly bashed some buttons into the navigation control and hoped for the best. It had mostly worked before. Mostly.

Stop. Chapter Time: Packed Launch

Helena and Jane stood at the command ships viewing portal to ensure the baggage handlers got the last of Helena's luggage on board. Even though hers was the only ship in the port, it hadn't stopped luggage being sent to the wrong solar system in the past. "OK lets voyage!" Helena declared as the last of the twenty HGV hover lorries dropped her travel luggage off (Helena having decided she would travel light for this mission).

As they walked away from the large viewing port Helena turner to Jane "You've recruited all the universes finest bounty hunters to our cause?" she asked.

Jane nodded eagerly "yes my queen, and some two-bob bounty hunters to make sure we got a good mix".

Helena considered this "Good, but if we find the glove first, make sure you cancel the standing order on the payments we made to them". Helena paused as she reached the lift up to the main decks, "Mind you, if I have the glove of power, I can do anything I want anyway. I'll just click their standing orders out of existence, that should save you some admin". Jane tried to hide her disappointment as Helena laughed to herself.

The lift reached the upper decks and Jane and Helena traversed the badly lit labyrinthine corridors, with the dangling wires, vent shafts and steam blowing from loose exposed pipes

"You know would it cost the royal purse that much to add a few more lightbulbs and tidy this up? It makes these corridors seem unnecessarily spooky, I mean fine if you were making a horror film, but its not very practical or good for the mood of people who are on the ship" Helena mused rhetorically.

Reaching Helena's royal chamber Helena strode to her throne, eased herself in and poured a drink from the mini bar in the arm rest. Jane took up her position on a small stool with a none too safe looking seatbelt duct taped to it. The fact that the stool wasn't fixed to the floor in any way troubled Jane considerably.

Helena leaned into the intercom in the arm rest of her chair "Commander, get us to Earth now".

"I'll try" a voice crackled back "but you've come through to the kitchen channel, you want channel five for the cockpit. Would you like a sandwich?"

Helena blushed "Sorry about that, I'll go through to channel five" she released her hand from the intercom, before pressing it again "And yes I'd love a sandwich please".

Helena then pressed the button for channel five "Captain?" Jane saw the look of relief on Helena's face as she'd clearly got the right channel this time (Helena as a royal not being used to the manual labour of pushing buttons). "Get us to Earth now please".

A deep rumbling built from the heart of the ship and the tannoy throughout the ship began a countdown "ten, nine…"

Helena took a slug of her highly alcoholic cocktail "You know I said we had to leave now, they could save us a little time on our journey by dispensing with the countdown".

"…eight, seven, six…"

Helena made sure her throne was in the upright position and picked up the manual on what to do in case sucked into a black hole, the advice seeming to be; hope for the best, but also keep your hopes low.

"…Five, four, three…"

Jane fished in her uniform for her travel sickness tablets and removed the paper bag stuck to the bottom of her stool.

"…three, oh sorry I said that one lift off…wait I mean two, one we are so outta here!"

And with that the wings on the command ship started flapping as the vessel prepared to meet its date with an Earthen destiny.

Chapter 10(?) - Planet Earth, and this is where the story really gets started. There is a bad moon on the rise.

Alex pulled at the office reception exit door. This was their first mistake, as it was a swing door. Realising their mistake, Alex tried to style it out by pretending to practice a kung fu move known as the 'drunkenly stumbling Andy Crane stance'. Alex looked around to see if anyone noticed and sure enough Claire and Salma and a host of people who had suddenly appeared from nowhere at the exact time to bask in Alex's stupidity. Claire and Salma were making a particularly huge deal of pointing and laughing at Alex. The gestures were so broad that even an amateur dramatics pantomime director would have vetoed them as 'a bit too much'.

Alex gave up the pretence and pushed through the door, the cold breeze that met them tasted like victory, well freedom certainly. Although some of that might have been the smell of the microwave meals on offer on the gourmet menu from the Waterside bar.

"When you two comedians have finished wetting yourself, are you coming to the pub with me?" Alex asked sharply as Salma and Claire emerged behind them.

"Would love to" Claire smiled "but its Tuesday and that's the night I sort my belly fluff collection. See you when you get in tomorrow mate". With that she patted Alex's back affectionately and strolled off. Alex let that familiar lurching feeling in their stomach go and turned to Salma.

"Fancy it Salma? I'm meeting Gaz and Steve-O in the Steamhouse. A night of high adventure waits"

"Well with an offer like that, it makes me want to give up my belief system and take up the drinking of warm flat beer. And as you've now mentioned those two were out my faith is being tested more than ever, but no I'm going to go home and watch Eggheads, at some point they'll stop getting the easier questions than the contestants and lose. Thanks, thought Alex". She turned and walked off towards the bridge that crossed the canal and tram lines.

"They do serve soft drinks. I think..." Alex muttered to themselves as they now stood alone on the waterside.

Ah well they were on their own and far from the first time, they would go meet up with Gaz and Steve-O, it wasn't like they were the worst company, well not quite, and it beat another night drinking on their own, that was always quietly a downer for Alex. Gaz and Steve-O worked on the other side of the council building, Alex regularly met them for a drink. It wasn't always their intention, but if you went for a beer in Sale, you had a 93.22(r)% chance of meeting them. These chances increased further if said day was one of the seven days in the week.

Gaz and Steve-O weren't so much bar flies as the results of two humans and two flies and the end four pumps on the bar undergoing some kind of freak teleportation accident. But with more beer involved. They had worked for the council longer than anyone could remember and the rumour that they simply materialised when someone read from an ancient haunted excel sheet found in the cellar of the building had yet to be disproved. They (very vocally) hated worked for the council but had found means of becoming un-sackable. This technique was known as 'limpeting' where they had been there that long that the cost and paperwork required to fire them was utterly prohibitive and no one was brave enough to take the task on. This meant their working day was a contradiction in terms and they whiled away the hours looking at videos of people falling over on the internet, before escaping to find the cheapest beer in a local bar, spending the night talking about the cheapest beer in that bar and how rubbish work was (as if they actually understood what the concept of the work they were supposed to do was). Truly they lived the dream.

Alex began to cross the concrete of the Waterside[51] when they were struck by a blinding flash "Bloody hell, some people will

---

[51] So called as it was essentially a patio next to a canal.

take pictures of anything[52]" Alex muttered to themself.

"My liege, tis an honour!" said a strange bearded man in a purple crushed velvet cloak appearing surprisingly suddenly in front of Alex. Alex regarded the man as dressing in the manner of someone in a failed glam rock band whose heart really wasn't in it. The bearded man hugged Alex like they were an old friend.

"The Wetherspoons is just over there mate." Alex said coldly "and I've no change I'm afraid.".

"No, thou doesn't understand" the bearded man continued "Tis vital I've found you, thou doth have a pivotal role in the safety of the galaxy. And there are larks to be had on the way" the man said earnestly grasping Alex by the shoulders and staring unevenly into their eyes.

Alex considered this, they were fond of that particular chocolate bar and that was about the only word they'd understood from this stranger. "Oh I see" Alex said, their sense of tedium rising "You're a Railway type of guy, figures. It's just around the corner, near the police station, handily."

"My capitan thy really must press…" the man was interrupted by a loud noise that sounded like a Vauxhall Nova backfiring and indeed looked like a Vauxhall Nova backfiring, but in

---

[52] As anyone who has seen regular picture of someone's plate of food posted regularly onto social media will attest to.

the sky. Alex saw the vehicle descend from above in a flash of dull brown. The vehicle landed on the concrete, bounced up, and straightened out its parking angle. The door counterintuitively raised up like a cockpit. Smoke billowed out as a hooded figure rose elegantly from their seat stepping out, before turning around and removing the keys from the ignition and putting the hand-break on.

"'Ere you can't park that spaceship there!" said an over officious voice from one of the office windows above. Probably a middle manager. Further in the background a traffic warden's eyes lit up, probably as a result of the carrot vindaloo curry they had consumed earlier.

The figure ignored the parking based advice and strode purposefully towards Alex with a (sports) casual menace. Alex found themselves taking a step back and try to stand behind the bearded stranger. The tall figure was now two paces from Alex and reaching into their glittery cloak for something. One pace now and their hand was rapidly coming up to Alex's face, Alex recoiled.

"Pick a card. Any card" said the figure holding up a deck of cards to Alex, the cards appeared to be monster truck themed. The figure pulled back their hood revealing an open smiling face. "it's a world beating trick this."

Chapter 11 (if the last one was 10) – a galaxy far away a long, long time ago

"We're out of bog roll!" bellowed Helena from the ship's royal crapper. "We're going to have to stop at a service station!".

Chapter 4: That's Narrator speak to a lady

The Narrator woke up on a hard surface a granite pillow digging into his face a blanket with the softness of plasterboard somehow failing to cover the entirety of their body no matter which way they turned it. Sitting up and seeing nothing but a bland purple he got his bearings, it came flooding back to him, he was in a Premier Inn on the planet Dirigible. The hotel was OK, just OK, an overbearing sense of being a kind of OK. With a bit of purple.

He took a sip of the tepid yellowish water to the side of his bed, he hoped it was water anyway. It came flooding back to him now, his self-appointed mission. He'd buggered up the intro to a very important story (probably turning people off getting this far) and he was going to put it right. He was going to find the protagonists and commentate on their every thought and manoeuvre, whether they thought that was annoying or not, certainly any protagonists he commentated on always got shirty with The Narrator when they went for a poo.

First, he had to find the heroes. This should have been easy, as the narrator, he knew how the story unfolded, unfortunately he'd left his copy of the story on the train and when enquiring at lost property he had been met with indifference bordering on the encounter causing existential angst in The Narrator. It was the age-old maxim of if you ring customer service and are met with utter disdain and there is no one there to hear your frustrations, are you actually making the phone call at all?

Still he remembered the story took part to a large degree in a glamourous Eldorado of a place called Sale, on planet Earth, so now all he had to do was get the thirty connections and seven overnight stays from his home in Belarus to get there. He couldn't help thinking the cheap tickets he'd booked used a route that was a little more circuitous than it needed to be.

The Narrator was going to put all storytelling wrongs right immediately, there was no time to lose, but first he had to eat five times his own body weight in toast[53] and preserves, he'd paid the extra for the all you can eat buffet and by gad he was going to make good on that £12 outlay. He'd also have to see how many of the mini muffins he could stuff into his pocket to snack on for the rest of the journey.

The intergalactic Megabus waited for no man. Woman. Child. Tentacled creature, or Were-Frog. Basically, the Megabus had a habit of pulling away when it saw people clearly running for its doors[54]. The Narrator would not fail the story again, well he hoped not, he'd give it a go and see what happened he guessed.

---

[53] Hats off to whoever saw a toaster and thought 'It's OK, but what we really need is for this bread to go on a conveyor belt journey a la the cart chase at the end of Indiana Jones and The Temple of Doom' for the toasting machine in hotels.
[54] A skill that must be in the job advert for most bus driving based roles.

Chapter here: Something wicked this way comes, aka getting your order fulfilled in in a Wetherspoons

Having had these two odd strangers thrust upon them, Alex decided there was nothing for it but to have a drink. One of these characters had protested strenuously at this course of action, though the other positively encourage as the best next step. So, not for the first time, democracy steered people into a terrible idea with hindsight.

Sitting in a quiet booth, Alex had been forced to consume too much information, and not enough alcohol in the last few minutes. And the card trick the strange woman had shown him had been rubbish, he could see she'd kept her thumb on his card to mark it.

Alex's two new associates sat opposite talking with great urgency and them throwing words around Alex didn't understand like; 'intergalactic gauntlet', 'prophecy', 'chosen one' and 'motivated'. Still they all agreed the ales they had ordered were passable.

"Look" Suzie (as she had revealed her name to be, again it was an average magic reveal at best) ventured "I could sit here drinking this ale all night…".

"…Good!" Alex and Zed (who deciding as it was a night for venturing names had given up his as well. He got 50p and half a bag of pork scratchings for it) interrupted simultaneously and turned to nod their heads appreciatively at each other and chink glasses.

"Burp!" Zed added for emphasis. Well not so much a belch as some kind of primal scream that shook the table and one of the nearby fruit machines giving the lucky punter/mug playing it a five pound return for their ten pound investment.

"You're lucky we found you first" Suzie carried on unperturbed. "if we know about you and this prophecy, you can guarantee the forces of evil will too. And some of them are really, really mean."

"How did you find me exactly" Alex asked, it dawning on them that was probably a question they should have asked earlier.

"Eashy Shire" Zed slurred, Alex was sure they'd only had quarter of their pint. "I ushed thou locashion update on Fashebook!" he waved his phone unsteadily in front of Alex.

"So wherever you're from, you have mobile phone technology and social media?" Alex asked.

"It's the mashive shpread of captialishm thy liege, they likesh to have a reach into everyesht market acrossh the sholar shsytems" Zed slurred conspiratorially, but also accurately.

"All considered, you should probably turn that off." Suzie counselled Alex looking at her intergalactic intercom[55] "and…oh for crying out loud 'Alex has checked into the J P Joule with a couple of weirdos, who dress like they've just found out about the practice of fancy dress without fully grasping the concept'. Did you write that while we were trying to explain to you the dire peril of your situation?" Suzie asked with just a hint of miff in her voice.

"Err…" Alex mumbled sheepishly. Could have been lambishly, it wasn't easy to gauge the age of his mumble.

"Look" Suzie began with a smile "turn that off now. You only leave it on in the quietly desperate hope that someone you fancy is in the same bar as you, sees the message and actually comes over to talk to you and yet that never happens does it?" This brutal message was delivered with Suzie's usual brightness and had the impact of being eaten by a shark whilst it gave you a back massage and told you were a unique delicate flower.

"Rerish!" said Zed unintelligibly.

"That's not true" Alex half-heartedly went on the defensive "look I've turned it off".

"OK" Suzie fixed Alex with her sternest look (which was about as stern as a baby rabbit playfully licking your eyeballs). "We need to get focused, we could be up against some…oh for f…'Alex is getting lectured by a manic pixie dream girl wannabe' give me that thing!" and so

---

[55] Like a mobile but with more buttons and a foot spa built in.

saying, Suzie grabbed Alex's phone and dropped it into Zed's pint, where it exploded into purple and green flame "ruddy hell!!" exclaimed Suzie. The contents of Zed's pint was best left to the guess of the curious chronic alcoholic.

"We need to find the glove and the only way we can do that is through the clues left by the ancient Quizzicals" Suzie declared.

Alex looked at Suzie Befuddledly "sorry the what?!"

"The – hic – Quizzicalsh my liege. They shet the cluesh to find the glove of power. Really hard cluesh, like The Guardian cryptic croshword." Zed fixed Alex with a smile "I love yoush!" and promptly fell (well it was more of a triple axel) backwards off his chair, which was especially impressive as it was a solid wall behind it.

"Luckily" Suzie picked up the (extremely frayed) conversational thread "I have the co-ordinates to the first clue location, I came to it by…err…well it doesn't matter how I came by it. It is at the following grid location which shows as here, its close so we can get it quickly and we're on our way" Suzie turned the phone to Alex to see the location, Alex nodded pretending that this all made total sense to them.

"I'll drinksh to that" Zed said clambering back to the table with all the effort of confronting K2. He produced a vial (vile?!) and dropped a pleasant-smelling orange liquid into everyone's glass. Zed wasted no time in necking his drink, broken bits of mobile phone and all.

Alex considered the swirling mass now churning in his drink "Why the hell not!" Alex necked the glass.

"Wait!! What about the clue? Oh, what the flip!" Suzie said beaten, draining her glass in one.

"Excelsior!" rallied Zed. At this point, all three passed into a slumped heap at the table and thusly they blended in seamlessly with the Wetherspoons regulars.

Intergalactic Planetary, but not on a planet. Or a planetarium or a plant factory, or at Robert Plants house

"Your highness" Jane started to bow, changed her mind, went for a curtsey, then giving it up as a bad lot, clicked her heels and winked. "exciting news, that...err...unforeseen...err...'space holes'...caused me to forget to mention earlier, but, anyway...I have a surprise!"

"I thought for a minute you'd forgot it's my birthday!" Helena said with a beam. A Jim Beam most likely judging by her wonky smile.

"What? oh yeah" Jane's tone remained neutral, as on Planet Eccles the royal family are needy enough to have an official birthday on 478 of the 475 calendar days. Generally, by the last official birthday, the street parties have been replaced with apathetically letting off a party popper at an elderly neighbour with a heart condition. "I'll give you your cake and present later." Jane said whilst sneakily ordering on her space phone a cake from Amazon Prime space cake section[56]. "No, your cakelessness, I mean gratefulness, this is something else."

"OK" said Helena indifferently, frankly she was suffering ennui. And it wasn't just the turps she had been drinking. She'd been in space for days now staring at an eternal canvas of stars

---

[56] One must be careful when ordering a space cake as if you order it from the wrong place its liable to make you 'sleepy' not long after consumption.

and was a little bored of everything. Even Jane's attempts at making 'insect robot wars' (an ant and earwig wrapped in foil fighting each other whilst a robotic simulation of Jonathan Pearce commentated) had resulted in her perk-o-metre reaching 'Hmmm' (slightly rising in cadence) at best.

Jane was not picking up on these vibes, but then she had never much been into percussion instruments. "Come with me your highness", Jane led Helena out of the royal chamber along the aforementioned straight dimly lit corridors of the ship to the science lab. The ship hadn't actually had a science lab, so they'd set up in the ship's gym, meaning most inventions the scientists had come up with were treadmill or weight based and of limited use. Though they had high hopes for the 'Grapes of Wrath O'bot' which would allow grapes to travel from one destination to another at a range of speeds and gradients.

Jane walked up to a tall standing structure covered in a gym towel. With a flourish Jane whipped the towel off "ta-da!" revealing a cross fit machine underneath. "oh, wait not that, sorry, over here" Jane said flushed. She moved to another tall structure covered in a towel, had a little peak under before removing the towel with much less of a flourish. "Behold the T10001! The latest in lean mean, fairly green Artificial Intelligence killing machine, it efficiently kills whilst learning your shopping habits."

In front of Helena was a tall, lithe, shiny, metallic exo-skeleton wearing what appeared to be a Hawaiian shirt fashioned out of brown paper and bubble wrap. The machine turned to face Jane eying her up with cold detachment whilst calculating the 5,051 different ways it could kill her with a blunt pencil. It then turned its inscrutable gaze on Helena. After a pause it opened its mouth to speak "Woah babes!" it said in a poor monotone robotic Keanu Reeves impression (on reflection, it wasn't that bad an impression).

"What the absolute flying f…" began Helena in shock, with a side salad of fury garnished with a hint of confusion.

"I think I can explain your highness." Began a nearby scientist, probably called Keith (the fact he wore a white lab coat just added to the sense of cliché). "You see the T10001, or tee one zero zero zero one, as we call him for short, is built to effectively assimilate all data and information available to it. Well, whilst I left it booting up, I think I left my laptop in with it. Recently, I've been studying early 1990's Earth surfer type films for scientific purposes, I've, err, yet to define, and well I think he's plugged into my laptop and watched these films and has taken onboard the style and language from these stories. I'm just grateful he went with these films and not the…errr…my top secret 'specialist' files on the computer." Keith looked from side to side at the room nervously.

"No way!" exclaimed the T10001.

"Soooo." Helena said pausing for breath, for fear if she did not she would hit this scientist over the head with his own colon, and not the punctuation mark type either. "This thing is going to kill all that's in its path whilst talking like a total idiot?"

"I believe so." Jane cut in seeing the scientist shrinking into himself so much he took on the properties of a prune in a vacuum bed. "Still" Jane continued "It could be a vital weapon in taking out all those do gooders and the person who may bring balance to the glove that I briefly mentioned to you whilst we were flying around in space not doing much."

"Right fine, great, what next?" Helena caught the room off guard with her sudden change in tone.

"Well" Keith came back in spotting an opportunity for redemption, like a worm a bird has dropped from its beak giving the bird a 'come and have another go if you think you're hard enough' gesture (not an easy gesture to perform if you're a worm, unless you're the Venezuelan Gesturio Worm). "Tee one…"

"GET ON WITH IT!" barked Helena, reminding the room her temper was as stable as a drunken ferret driving a motorbike down a particularly winding road on an icy day.

"Yes get on with it!" barked the crew of the ship in chorus too.

"It's impervious to numerous hostile conditions in space and virtually indestructible, so essentially we can put him in a torpedo tube and fire him at Earth, enabling him to arrive before us as a kind of advance party. The tube reaches temperatures of over 10,000 degrees centigrade and smells of eggy farts, but Tee will be ok".

"Do it!" ordered Helena "And get me gin. And something to punch!".

"Bummer." Said T10001.

Chapter: Onward Slow Ignoble Steed

The Narrator found himself a seat on the bus by the window and got comfy. The bus was reasonably quiet with everyone having a spare seat next to themselves. The bus started to pull away and The Narrator relaxed. At this point a red faced overweight man appeared on the bus having just made it at the last minute, the man scanned around for a seat, The Narrator tried to make himself looks as fierce as possible, but to no avail this fierce look had more resemblance to a startled young squirrel watching 2001 a Space Odyssey.

With great inevitability the man sat next to The Narrator and began to fully spread out unspooling like a badly packed suitcase falling off a car roof rack onto the motorway, pinning The Narrator to the window. The Narrator could feel the mini muffins being crushed in his pockets and sighed louder than he intended.

The overweight man then pulled out a tablet device and set it up on the fold down table in front of him, further trapping The Narrator with the wire from the tablet to his headphones. This was going to make using the bus toilet near impossible for The Narrator, however he wasn't sure he was foolhardy enough to brave that infernal contraption anyway.

The overweight man[57] lastly produced a large spicy lamb, blue cheese, egg, pickled Monster Munch and Balti chicken sandwich from his

---

[57] He has a name you know, though I don't know what it is.

coat pocket along with a packet of scampi fries and proceeded to eat noisily, messily and loudly.

Hunched up against the window The Narrator held in the silent scream pouring from the centre of his being at the prospect awaiting him for the next thirty hours. All in all, this coach journey was going slightly better than normal.

Chapter Below – Is there life on Mars? And does it have more sense than to listen to Slade at Christmas?

Alex awoke atop a wide mountain ledge, mist swirled hiding the oblivion that surrounded the rocky outcrop. Around Alex lay two monoliths minding their own business, truth be told. A light that was somehow dull yet illuminating hung in the air, like a cliché looking for another story.

In front of Alex around a low fire stood a cowled figure tending to the flames with a twig, the occasional flicker sending sparks up revealing for a split-second features that seemed familiar, but Alex couldn't place, within the hood.

Behind Alex a red sun began to set as a yellow sun somehow simultaneously rose in the opposite direction. A further blue sun had taken the day off miffed at the sun based overcrowding.

"Wh-wh-where am I[58]?" Alex asked the figure groggily.

"You are nowhere!" barked the figure stealing a line from the excellent Big Trouble in Little China (you can't blame them for that really).

"Ah come on now!" pressed Alex "I have to be somewhere."

---

[58] No one coming to ever gets that sentence right in one take

"It's clearly a dream sequence you numbskull" sighed the figure wearily.

"Oh."

The figures gaze didn't leave the fire. It was getting a bit too hot for their face, but they had decided this was the most enigmatic pose for them, so they were just going to have to tough out the burning they were feeling in their cheeks. "To meet your destiny, you must draw from within".

Alex took a moment to soak that in. Nope they didn't get it. "What does that mean?" they asked.

"I don't know!!" began the figure their voice an octave higher than previously. "The first rule of being a mentor type figure is you speak in unhelpful riddles that resolve themselves at the end of the adventure. 'Your true self will save the universe'. That's all I've got"

"Any chance, you could bend the rules and give me, you know, something useful?" Alex asked, not unreasonably they thought.

"No!" snapped the figure.

"Who are you then?" Alex tried another what they felt was a fair question.

"I am everyone. No one. I know you well." The figured mused after a pause.

Alex was giving up at this point. "So how do I get home oh utterly unhelpful sod one?" they tried.

"I told you it's a dream. How do you escape a dream?"

Alex paused to think. "Erm, wet the bed?"

The figure totally ignored Alex's logic pattern. "Before you go, take this, you will know when to use it.". The figure passed Alex an object. Alex inspected the item, it was a cheap rip off of a swiss army knife, without any of the cooler features. It might have had the toothpick.

"OK smart arse. If this is a dream how do I even take it with me and use it?" Alex asked a rather good question for them.

"Second rule of mentoring. It's all very simple you just have to…" and with that they pinched Alex forcing them to wake and leave this plane. "Phew!" said the figure pulling their head away from the fire and rubbing their face.

Alex felt themselves coming out of their sleepy stupor. Reaching into their pocket, they felt something hard. Shocked, Alex pulled the object out and discovered it was the cheese and pickle sandwich they'd put in there four days ago. Alex examined the matter in front of them and after getting over their initial terror, filed it under 'M' for 'Maybe later' and slipped it back into their pocket.

Putting their hand into the other pocket Alex felt another object which definitely had the right consistency to be a swiss army knife. With that Alex decided that was enough for now and a bit more sleep was in order and drifted off again to see if they could persuade the fireside figure to speak straight and, you know, actually help them out.

Chapter Chapter – Needing a little thinking time

The thinker stared from his window into the vastness of space beyond the cottages over the road. Forever examining all the timelines for what will be, has been and could be, and with a little more effort from some lazy people, might actually be. How was this quest for the glove of power going to end? The Thinker saw so many options good and ill, the twin imposters he'd learnt to treat fairly alike.

Personally, he was hoping the battle for ownership of the glove was going to end with the rocket pack dinosaurs saving the day at the last moment, that always made for a good end of the many quests he'd watched play out before.

Mostly the thinker was thinking about that just past best yoghurt in his fridge and if it was still edible, alas the weaves of time were giving him nothing on that.

The Thinker noticed his neighbour, The Talker coming out of the cottage over the road, and quickly drew the curtains. The Thinker didn't like the Talker, his constant babbling ruined his meditations. The Thinker wasn't that keen on his other neighbour The Doer either. Far too energetic. The Thinker wasn't a lot of fun at parties.

The Thinker took his thoughts off the constant lines of fate and settled into some of his greatest hits of thinking; how his seeing of the future has never won him the lottery, or avoided bank holiday traffic, or how to spot the 48.7 signs of aging that only an expensive face cream can cure, How Olly Murs became a thing[59] and why he can't answer Annie Lennox when she sings "Tell me whyyy-yyy-yyy, whyyy-yyy-hhhyyyy whyyyy-hyyy"?. The Thinker was thinking of going to sit on the toilet to do some serious pondering, he'd had some of his greatest revelations there[60].

These musings were interrupted by his wife Gemma T Thinker coming into the room. "Dwayne, what do you want from the shops for your tea?" she snapped.

"Lady, I am musing the fates of the universe, I need to see where the twists of time will take us, to foresee and prevent the forces of darkness subjugating sentient life to an eternity of suffering and stuff like that." The Thinker said a little pompously, especially as he didn't tend to take much action on these matters when he saw it anyway.

"Every day you're doing that, and where has it got us?! Eh? Eh?!" Gemma probed, annoyed "Its not like you ever do anything about it is it? You just sit there all smug for days when you watching something leads to you calling it right.

---

[59] In the future hopefully that name inspires the reaction "who he?". And by the future that would ideally be any time in the next week or so.
[60] Who knows why, thems just the rules.

What good is that to anyone? It doesn't change anything!".

"Well…" The Thinker went to speak, not his strong suit.

"No, don't give me that, you've never thought about getting a proper job?! Or doing a little housework eh? And who is it keeping us fed?! My mum was right about you, feckless she said, feckless! And yet I put up with you, god knows why, have the fates told you that eh? Why I put up with you?!" She glowered at The Thinker her arms folded tightly across her chest.

The Thinker went to answer the final rhetorical question before realising the folly of such an action. "Could I have cheese and onion pie for tea please?" He asked. What The Thinker really wanted was a neurological recorder so he could record all the timelines and watch the highlights later, giving him time to watch Bargain Hunt in the day, but he wasn't going to push his wife for that today.

"Fine OK." Gemma said brightening a fraction. "And while I'm out, I'll enquire at the Supermarket if there are any jobs going for you. I think you'd make a half decent shelf stacker." And with that, she left the room.

The Thinker slumped into his armchair. He was trying unsuccessfully to see if the fates would reveal how successful his wife would be in getting him that blasted job.

This page is left intentionally blank[61]

---

[61] And by including that sentence the page is rendered intentionally not blank.

89

Chapter 14(?) Back to the Ship Shop as sung by Sean Connery featuring backing vocals from Sylvester Stallone, Susan Sarandon and Sharon Stone

"Your Highness?" Jane poked her head around the door of the royal chamber. This was especially difficult as the doors were automatic, so Jane had to get her timing spot on running at the doors at a sprint and then dodging to the side at the last moment to peer in. Jane looked at Helena attempting to gauge her mood. It looked somewhere between dark and a Manchester winter skyline.

"Oh for flips sake!" it seems the royal HR department had got to Helena, warning her that swearing wasn't good for staff morale. "I was nailing a really tough soduko". Jane saw Helena put the book down. Jane could see on the page there was a couple of numbers in boxes (one appeared to be the number 25) with a lot of crossing out in them.

"I have good news?" Jane said uncertainly, using her best upper diphthong, which really showed off the buttocks in her speech pattern. "We've been having a think amongst the team and we were figuring the rocket side car isn't really getting used, nor is that legion of your finest troops that are hanging around in the store cupboard boxing up the Royal souvenir mugs and bed spreads. We could maybe send them ahead in the side car as a kind of vanguard?".

"So, we have an elite army on board and the means of getting them to the planet Earth ahead of us?" Helena asked, her tone uneasy to work out.

"Yes."

"Combined with that irritating 'bot, I only found out about a couple of days ago. Who should probably be at Earth by now."

"Yes."

"Hmm. It seems like something of an oversight that we're only finding out about these things half way through the journey that would have been very useful at the start." Helena picked up her Suduko book and seemed to scrawl something within the pages.

"Yes your highness, it definitely seems like a large mistake…" Jane stared at the ground though the ground seemed unwilling to grant her the swallowing up she was after. "I'll make some further checks to make sure there are no other gaping misses that would get this quest speeded up."

Chapter All Hail Sale!

Alex was moving in and out of consciousness, in and out just a little like a cat stood in the doorway wanting to go out to the toilet but aware it's raining ever so slightly. Actually, it was nothing like that. Like that cat in the misfiring metaphor, Alex was close to weeing where they were. Forcing their eyes open and letting in the pain that entailed, Alex saw that they were on the raised patio of a beer garden surrounded by bin bags and two other prostrate figures. Alex was all too aware, suddenly, of a presence looming over them.

"Rise and shine slug a bed!" said the figure in a sing song sort of voice. Alex was taking time to process all this, who was this new figure, who were the two they got roaringly drunk with the other night, what did the dream with the strange figure tell them? And what the hell does slug a bed mean anyway?

"Bleeeuuughhh!" said a stirring figure next to Alex. Actually, it might have been "Blleeeeuuugghh!".

Alex heavily pushed themselves into the sitting position at considerable pain, seeing Zed opposite, stood up and smiling taking in the new day with wonder. Alex's hand dropped by onto the floor they felt something cold, spinning it Alex could feel it was an unopened bottle of beer. Alex picked it up and examined it. With a triumph shout of "Aha!" they reached into their pocket and produced the pocket knife flipping the bottle opener out they cracked the top of the beer off "Success, hair of the dog!", Alex's triumph caught in their throat as the new figure knocked the beer out of their hand sending it and the contents scattering. Alex caught Zed's gaze and a look of horror in his eyes at what he had just witnessed.

"What day is it?" Alex asked trying to hide the disappointment in their voice.

"Never mind that, what ruddy eon is it?!" Suzie chimed as she slowly rose to her feet. Every syllable caused a pound in her head.

"It's Friday" said the stranger "2021, if it helps?". Alex felt the stranger go behind them link their arms under Alex's armpits and lift them up as if they weighed the same as the brain of a UKIP[62] MP.

"But that means we lost three days!" wailed Suzie, a note of panic (C#m – a good note for panic) in her voice. "We only have one more day before the moon rises revealing the whereabouts of the glove!"

"You really overdid the juice huh?" Asked the figure a mocking tone in their voice.

"Who are you?" Alex finally got around to asking the obvious question. They turned to face the stranger.

---

[62] We can only hope that what UKIP was quickly gets lost in the annuls of time and this reference makes no sense to future readers.

"I am…it's probably best you call me Luci. With two C's." the stranger smiled brightly at Alex and gave a graceful little bow.

After a long pause (polar bear sized almost) Suzie spoke "What do you want from us?".

"My job is to prevent the glove falling into evil hands, pun not intended. I believe you all have a similar quest, don't ask me how I know this, it's a long story, you'll just have to accept I'm good at figuring these things out. You'll need my skills. Trust me." She reached her arm out and lent on the wall taking in the three figures a smirk playing across her face. This smirk quickly faded as her arm slipped on the wall and she nearly fell on her face.

"How could thoust knoweth all that?" Zed asked, an impressed tone in his voice.

"I did say not to ask, but since you did anyway, I got advanced copy from a train seat." Was all Luci would say in response.

"Well I've got the co-ordinates for the first clue to the glove so lets get on it" Suzie said holding the sides of her head in a failed attempt to make it less painful to speak.

Luci nodded and breezily walked away before any further inevitable follow up questions were asked of her. Groggily two of our heroes followed Luci (though they probably should have followed Suzie given she had the clue), whilst the third considered the spilt beer on the floor, began to kneel, thought better of it and headed off after them.

"Wait!" Alex shouted. Luci spun to regard them, then thought disregarding might be the better option. "Why me? Why am I the one that needs to find this, glove thing you all keep banging on about?"

"As you were foretold in the inevitable prophecy" Luci shot back.

"Oh no. I'm not having that prophecy crap! I want a legitimate reason." Alex stated pausing in his following of everyone.

Suzie sighed, turning and facing Alex they squeezed their shoulder. "You must know. Basically, the glove gives ultimate power to its wearer. What with total power corrupting totally, we needed a figure of…a person who could" Suzie took in a deep breath "…we needed the laziest least motivated person in the universe. The scriptures pointed to you." She squeezed Alex's shoulder again and gave him a smile.

"What?!" Alex asked incredulous with a little indignace to get the balance right.

"Well I say the scriptures, we basically ran an algorithm on your LinkedIn page". Suzie met Alex's look in the eyes "Basically, you were seen as so lacking in any motivation that even with all that power you wouldn't be bothered to do anything to place the universe in danger, well bother to do anything full stop. Thusly the universe would be safe from someone with a little more gumption trying to get the glove to do nefarious things." She snorted and turned to carry on walking.

"Tis true my liege" Zed confirmed. "Thou is lazier than the stoner sloth from the planet Snooze."

"Lazier than the sociology student doing as essay on the media's portrayals of corporate crime." Luci added with a chuckle.

"I'll show you motivation." Alex muttered "Give me that glove and I'll be kicking you guys into shape".

"No you won't! Besides, you're gonna kick us into shape? What are you gonna do, put the glove on your foot?" Suzie was openly laughing now. "Now where are those co-ordinates? We haven't a moment to lose. Again."

Chapter anew: The Immigration game

The Narrator stood in the queue at customs to get through the toll to planet Earth. After the interminable bus journey, the feeling was slowly returning to his legs, but currently he was walking like an elderly penguin that had overdone the Espresso Martinis. His mind was still numb from the horrors he had been through on the journey.

The Narrator was twenty-five hours behind schedule, he knew, just knew, he was going to get held up in the traffic of the space port city of B1RM-1NG-4AM. The last 15 hours of the journey had been rough, the overweight man had left the bus and just as The Narrator was getting comfortable a family with four children took all the seats around him. This in itself wasn't too much of a problem, but when one of the children threw up all the Bariho Starmix they'd been eating, the sickly sweet smell had made for a rough journey, especially when this mixed in with the abomination someone had left in the bus toilet. This combined smell was going to take years of therapy for The Narrator to forget.

The Narrator found themselves at the front of the queue for immigration. "Next!" barked the brown shirted officer in front of him, The Narrator strode confidently forward.

"Err Hello" The Narrator smiled kindly at the officicer being met with a (dry) stone wall face that was playing with the idea of moving to a class one snarl.

"Name?"

"Arron. Arron Rhatte," The Narrator tried another smile which had all the impact of catapulting a toasted marshmallow at a castle wall in the middle of a medieval siege.

"Purpose of Visit" the immigration officer asked in a low monotone rumble.

The Narrator had a think on this one, how to call it, attempting to help save the universe? Providing commentary to those trying to save the universe? Universe overseer? "I'm on a lobster spotting holiday" was what he blurted out. He wasn't sure where it came from, but it seemed the quickest way through at the time.

The immigration officer stared at The Narrator, causing the Narrators bowels still delicate from the scent of sweet vomit to drop a little. "Occupation?" he growled with a hint of menace.

The Narrator was on firm footing here and he knew it "Narrator!" he said with pride drawing himself up to his full height and nearly toppling over as his legs didn't quite have the feeling for the task yet.

"Hmm" was all the officer could manage, keying something into the computer terminal in front of them. After an inordinately long pause the officer looked up from their computer terminal

"Nope!", the officer folded his arms across his chest and looked at The Narrator.

"Sorry, nope what please sir?" The Narrator asked not unreasonably.

"We don't have Narrator in our list of occupations allowed into Earth. It's not a priority job, so I can't let you in." the officer added nothing further to their explanation.

"But I'm not stopping sir, I'm not intending to work either" The Narrator decided a little lie here was probably safe "it's just a short break, I've travelled all this way to see the wonderful lobsters of Earth?" The Narrator pleaded. The officer thrust a form, no form undersells it, a novel (and not a short one with small words in a big font that is easy to read) of paper into The Narrators chest.

"You want to have a holiday on Earth? You need to complete the WoFT 57845 form." The officer pointed at a bench and table behind The Narrator and walked into the back office offering no more guidance.

The Narrator trudged to the seats taking a moment to look out of the portal window as a bearded man riding a unicycle hyper tortoise sped through space outside "bloody hipsters" the narrator muttered.

48 hours, 57 minutes and 42 seconds[63] later The Narrator finally completed the form to the

---

[63] Just under the time the advice on the Government website states that you will need to complete the form.

immigration officials satisfaction and he was on the jet bus heading to Earth wondering why he hadn't given up on the poxy story about saving the universe several weeks ago.

Chapter whatever; Space isn't Ace

"I spy with my little eye something beginning with 'S'" Jane said brightly, whilst staring out of the royal chamber portal[64]. Helena shuddered and slumped into her throne, burying her head in her hands. Her hands proving not deep enough for Helena's internment needs.

I Spy may be the most tedious game ever, but you should try it in the confines of space, once you've got 'S' for 'Star' and 'B' for 'Blackhole' and also 'B' for 'Bottytron from the planet Urhairyanus' out of the way it gets a tad repetitive, and suddenly the possibility of being jettisoned into the unforgiving vacuum of the galaxy seems inviting. If indeed it wasn't inviting the moment you started to play.

"How far are we from Earth?" Helena asked impatiently.

"That doesn't begin with 'S' your highness!" Jane rebuked Helena with as much strength as a supermarket brand teabag dipped in tepid water.

"Justanswerthebloodyquestion!!" Helena spat back, her head fractionally raising from her hands, thinking better of it and lowering back in.

"Not far your highness. Just over the next black hole and around the dark matter one-way

---

[64] Essentially the same as a standard port hole, but with gilding, because you know, royalty stuff...

system." Jane smiled giving an answer vague enough to appease her leader. She hoped.

Helena sighed wearily. "I'm going stir crazy Jane". Helena gazed around the imposing chamber a glazed look on her face "stuck on this poxy ship, with a load of numb nut lackies – present company very much included – living in a cramped cabin with not enough space to swing a rocket pack cat in, and I should know cos I've tried!"

"Space! You got it!" Jane beamed at Helena.

"What?!" Helena asked, a question she feared she'd rue learning the answer to.

"That was my I Spy – space - you got it!"

Helena slumped her head on the table (an impressive feat given it was a full ten feet from the throne). Gently sobbing, she prayed for a critical breach in the ship's hull.

Chapter 9 – The not so Fantastic Four

"Are you sure it's here?" Luci asked as they stood outside the Co-Op in Sale town centre. A none descript mini market type of building. Stick your head out of the window, you'll probably see the like near you.

"Like, the hips, the co-ordinates never lie!" Suzie confirmed digging back into pop music of the early 2000's to make her point, an approach that brooked no argument, though she did have Hot in Herre by Nelly as back up, just in case.

"Nothing for it est" Zed said drawing his cape close to him, seemingly motivated by something, probably not having had a drink for an hour. He was staying true to the Turpin family motto of 'soonest started, soonest buggering off to the pub'. "I did not know thou hast magic on your world." Zed said admiringly as the automatic door pulled back for him "impressive thy impressive".

"OK we split up!" Alex declared, surprised at their own pro-activeness. "Zed take the beer and crisps section." Alex did a quick sideways glance and saw Zed salivate "No Suzie beer and crisps, Luci toiletries, I'll take the fridges and Zed...err...fresh vegetables". Zed looked baffled, it wasn't so much he didn't understand the words fresh and vegetables as the concept. All four went to put their hands in for some kind of break, realised they hadn't practiced and thus tottered off to deal with their part of the search.

Alex strolled down the sandwich aisle noting the vast variety of vegetarian sandwiches; egg, egg and cress, cheese, cheese and onion and the extremely exciting and exotic, cheese ploughman's (cheese with lettuce *and* pickle guaranteed to be limp and soggy, what a time to be alive and not eat meat). Next came the drinks, including the excessively priced health drinks, which had all the health benefits of a weekend on the town with a time travelling 1970s Keith Richards who had a bionic liver fitted and was just coming out of having done a month of staying sober for charity.

The first day of the adventure and this quest was already proving tedious and the drinking the night before had left Alex with a pounding head, they should have taken the aspirin aisle with hindsight. Or failing that black aspirin[65].

Somewhere on another aisle Suzie let out a "A-ha!" of delighted declaration. Well it may have been an ordinary declaration, but the intonation definitely went up at the end implying an upbeat declaration. The four companions vectored in on her vocal co-ordinates. Alex rounded the corner, they were thinking of squaring the corner, but settled on the

---

[65] A can of coke a drink with that much sugar the rush removes any feeling of hangover for about 4 minutes and 29 seconds.

traditional means at the last moment, as it seemed the respectful thing to do.

Suzie was stood looking at the shop notice board (becoming the first person to look at it since Mildred Goggins on 4th January 1971 who was looking for someone to walk her Ferret, Alfonso). All four of our heroes reached Suzie at the same time, what with a Co-Op being an easy place to traverse, unless you get stuck behind someone checking each individual tin of tuna to see which is the most appetising.

"You see…?" Suzie asked a little smugly. Smug didn't fit Suzie too snug(ly).

"Now waiteth my good lady" Zed started "the Quizzicals have the sharpest most cunning minds in the known (and some parts of the unknown) universe, and their fiendish riddles are known to drive some of the finest (and unfinest) minds close to insanity (and sanity)…"

"…of for f…" Luci began, as at this point our heroes had given up on finishing sent…

"…What? WHAT?!" Alex asked desperately, not sure what they were supposed to be seeing.

"Look!" Luci said matter of factly, with a soupcon of irritation.

"I'm not seeing it." Alex stated trying to hide the panic in their voice.

At this point, Luci grabbed Alex's head and thrust it to the centre of the notice board so fast Alex nearly forgot to take their brain with them. "Ah I see." Alex said satisfied.

"Do you?!" Luci snapped back.

"Err…"

"There!" Luci pointed so hard at the notice board one of the drawing pins considered telling her it was rude but thought better of it seeing the anger etched on her face.

"Oh…" Alex said, their voice tailing off. In the centre of the notice board (next to a card place by Agents Bailey and Turner requesting help finding demons, vampires and sasquatches), in a neon envelope with 'First clue to the gauntlet to rule the World. Ta, The Quizzicals' written on it. The envelope was surrounded by four glittery arrows with fairy lights attached pointing at it. Just to be on the safe side, the Quizzicals had set up a recording of a pleasant accompanying ditty with the lyrics:

"You searched long and hard
For the first clue
Now pick up the envelope containing the card
And find out what to do"

"Pathetic" muttered Luci darkly to no one in particular.

"Agreed m'lady" Zed nodded "A blatant musical rip off of 'Live and Let Diest'.

Alex turned their head to their left at the young staff member picking their nose behind the counter "That song not irritate you?".

"Eh?" said the shopworker, before reaching down to the counter below and pick a packet of sweets to eat. On realising he'd accidently picked up a pack of cough sweets, he simply shrugged and proceeded to open the packet and greedily chew away.

Alex turned back to see Suzie now had the envelope in her hands and was fingering it nervously. Zed had taken a step back and was repeating the words "fiendish, fiendish." With a look of rapt admiration on his face. Luci continued to look puce with anger. It wasn't her colour and certainly was doing nothing to compliment her choice of lipstick shade, but many a person struggles to co-ordinate their lipstick choice on an estimate of how angry they will get in a day.

"OK, her goes!" Suzie smiled, then cleared her throat "exciting eh?" she spun the envelope around in her fingers a few times and blew on it for good luck, held it to the light to see what may be in it, then gave it a good shake "never can be too careful eh?" she chuckled. She then waggled it a few times. A large pause then, err, enveloped. The three others stared at her confused.

"I um…don't know how to open an envelope!" Suzie admitted with a hint of wail. Seeing the look of astonishment on her companions faces she blurted "We use carrier star emus from where I'm from!".

Luci snatched the envelope from Suzie disdainfully. She drew her cape back and pulled an elaborate letter opener with a humorous anteater shaped handle, from her belt. "I got that from Costa Del Sol 7[66]" she said with a look of happy nostalgia playing across her face. She sliced the letter open with a worrying grace and efficiency. Inside was a postcard, a slightly blue one from Blackpool by the looks of it. "Ready?" not waiting for a response she ploughed on.

*"Roses are red, Violets are blue
Here is your first clue
My first is in wavy and wet
My second rhymes with 'day' but begins with a w instead
My third some eat with fish, some have on their shoulder
My fourth is the same as where you are stood now
My fifth is, I don't have a fifth."*

"Genius!" Zed declared his eyes closed in some kind of rapture.

"OK so we have four words" Luci declared.

"Well its obviously the four words Sea. Way. Chip. Shop." Suzie contributed feeling much

---

[66] A planet where every exotic restaurant sells egg and chips to make sure the English don't panic.

better within herself now the pressure of opening envelopes was off.

"My lady, how doth thou be so sure?" Zed asked with astonishment.

"Because the clues are bleedin' obvious!" Luci chipped in. Zed found himself nodding despite himself.

"Sea way chip shop mean anything to you Alex?" Suzie said fixing a stare on them. Alex scrunched their face up, looked up, squinted their eyes, but just couldn't settle on the right face to convey 'thinking hard'. "Sea way chip shop?" Suzie repeated in a soothing tone.

"This!" Luci had already Googled[67] it and held her phone uncomfortably close to Alex's face.

"Oh, the *Seaway* Chip shop. Yeah, it's also in Sale, I was there last Friday!" Alex said with triumph in their voice, totally failing to see the look of disgust on everyone else's face. "Don't eat the chips though. Not unless you have an iron gut. The damage that place can cause the next day" Alex cautioned with a serious tone.

"To Ashton Village!" Luci declared with a hint of excitement having used Google to know that Ashton Village was part of Sale, that Alex had just referred to.

"How do you know it's there?" Alex asked blankly.

---

[67] Other internet search engines are available. And may not be spying on you.

"That clue? the Google page? I just…oh look forget it…" Luci gave up.

"Thou can use thy rocket ship!" Zed declared to cheers from the others.

With that our heroes skipped out of the shop except for Luci who decided to hop out to break up the symmetry. Behind the counter the shop worker began to nibble on the wad of tissues he'd accidently just picked up from the counter below them.

Chapter happening - The Space Race Chase not featuring Ace of Bass, Mace (Windau), The A-Team's Face, Black Lace or Hale and Pace.

"Here?" Jane asked taking a step back, a hint of nervousness in her voice.

"Yeah, whatever" Helena said distantly. Jane placed the cooking apple on her head.

"Err, isn't it me who is meant to wear the blindfold?" She asked with a hint of desperation in her voice.

"Don't you know the Earthen legend of William Tell?" Helena responded. Jane wasn't sure any of this matched the William Tell stories she'd read, and she had read a surprising lot on Earthen legends for someone born a long way from that planet.

"I'm pretty sure he didn't use a plasma bazooka though your highness" Jane reasoned.

"He lacked ambition!" Helena countered again. She primed the device, dropped the blindfold over her eyes and span around four times to make the whole thing more interesting.

"What if you completely miss and breach the ship?" Jane tried a different tact.

"Meh." Helena gave the question zero thought, she really wasn't bothered about anything in particular right now. She lifted the bazooka in the direction of roughly Jane (whoever roughly Jane was). Or so she thought. Whatever.

"My Queen." Said Captain Justin Time (his actual name) entering the chamber through the sliding doors.

"Of for f…" Helena began, before muttering "…think of staff morale, think of staff morale" under her breath, before finally settling on "What news do you have captain?". She continued to impatiently play with the safety catch on the bazooka.

"T10001 has made contact, he's just about to reach Earth!" Captain J Time declared feeling pleased to deliver good news.

"Really?" Helena raised a genuinely interested eyebrow to compensate for her genuinely disinterested eyebrow. "What was his status report?"

"Ah, well…you see…" The Captain spluttered "…I struggled to understand the message in its entirety. There was definitely a 'rad' in there, maybe a 'bodacious' or two, he may even have thrown in a 'Cowabunga'…plus there was a bit of static on the line, so the message wasn't one hundred percent clear. Its definitely good news though."

"Lord help us" Helena muttered to herself "Anyway good news is good news. Jane, get us a translator that speaks pure 90's Terran idiot, we need to fully understand that infernal engine." Helena began to lower the bazooka using her off hand to force the weapon down against her will as Jane let out a breath that lasted longer than some successful American TV series.

Here be a chapter - As high as a skunk kite

"Behold!" Zed declared as he led his companions from the Aldi staircase onto the carpark above where Zed's ship lay parked badly across four parking bays. It was still parked better than the Audi 4x4 in the bay across from it.

The group had agreed that speed was of the essence and Zed's ship was that essence of speed, though that wasn't its actual name. The vessel looked like an owl made of paper mâché. That is an owl designed by the dream team of the ghost of Picasso, a particularly uncreative and Ritalin addled six-year-old, an artistic but temperamental field mouse called Graham and an amateur rugby team many pubs into stag do.

Alex walked over to the off-white structure and inspected it carefully. It was *actually* made of paper mâché. "'And now I have to something something dogs for Quavers'" Alex read an obscured newspaper headline on the ship. Two other headlines they could make out were 'All foreigners are dangerous and want your jobs and to undermine your Britishness' and 'Women in positions of power are unnatural and scary and they must be undermined to protect their own prettiness'. Clearly, they got the Daily Mail on planet...planet, whatever the hell planet Zed was from.

Zed sauntered around the back of the vessel and pressed the green button marked 'this one openeth the doors'. The ramp at the back dropped at alarming speed until it got halfway down, at which point it started to go up again, before finally deciding down was the way for it to go, gently reaching the ground with a satisfied 'pfft' sound, smoke billowing out from within. Zed stepped up the ramp.

The three companions who weren't Zed looked at each other with curiosity before ascending the ramp behind him.

Inside, the ship was a pristine chrome full of lights and buttons that screamed 'high tech', you know the sort, the type that includes the lights that move up and down in sequence for no discernible reason. "siteth, siteth" Zed said gesturing to some sofas that were to the back of the cockpit.

Alex chose 'chair foureth' (as it was helpfully labelled), before pulling on a seatbelt (racing style no less). Luci and Suzie took up seats close by. Zed eased himself into the pilot seat at the front and did up the seatbelt before checking his mirrors were all aligned and switching the heating on the back window.

"Will you start the fans please?" he began then followed with "start retro thrusters!" Zed casually flicked a switch, the ship responded with a low thrum. "Start future thrusters!" Zed flicked another switch, and the ship harmonised its hums. "Hiteth the 'Let's do this' button!" he declared pressing the appropriately labelled button. Zed sat back looking very pleased with himself. Everyone waited for something to happen. After a few minutes, Suzie took it on herself to speak for everyone and leant forward towards Zed.

"Can we fly there now please Zed?" she asked gently with an encouraging smile.

"Eh-eth?" Zed seemed uncertain to what the question was driving at and the question was a considerate driver.

Staying her usual sweet self and speaking fast before the other two could undo their seatbelts to get up and smack Zed around the back of the head "You know, can you fly your ship so that we can get to the next location to complete the next part of our quest. Please?"

"My lady this ship doesn'teth fly." Zed said in what he thought was a reasonable tone.

"Well, however it moves, can we get it moving to the Village?" Suzie pressed just managing to keep her tone positive.

"My good Queen, thy vessel doth not move." Zed seemed confused at the line of questioning. Though he remained upbeat.

"But when we said we needed to get there you suggested using your sodding ship!" Alex interjected.

"I do, and we're on itly. Splendineth isn't it? It doth not move though" Zed's tone again suggested he didn't understand the fuss.

"But it was implicit we were to travel by it…what about the wings…all the buttons you pressed…?! Suzie stumbled over her questions before settling on "How the ruddy heck did you get here in it?!" even her positive frame of mind dampened.

"Oh, I got towed by my friend Pat who was comingeth this way" Zed said with a kindly smile. Defeated the three others undid their seatbelts, stood up and got off the ship gazumped so much that violence to Zed was beyond them. Even Luci.

"Its OK its not a problem" Suzie smiled "We can take my space Nova there, it will be a squeeze, but it will work."

The three rushed down the car park steps up School Road precinct[68] crossed past the town hall and came back the waterside where Suzie had first shown Alex a rubbish magic trick.

As they closed in on Suzie's spaceship her hands went up to her face in anguish "Noooo!" she wailed.

"OK" Alex stated phlegmatically "that one I can explain" they said nodding to the wheel clamp on the front tyre of Suzie's vessel "that one is more of a mystery" Alex said indicating to the clamp that had been attached to the thrusters to the rear of the vehicle to prevent take off. "When I have the glove of power I'll magic

---

[68] The perfect place to go shopping if you like pound bakeries, charity shops and bookies and…no just those things.

those off, or whatever it is this glove does, you've probably told me. Either way, your ship isn't getting us to the village I'm afraid Suzie."

"I'm getting a taxi there." Luci announced after a little consideration.

"Can't afford it, bus for me." Alex chipped in with a slight groan in their voice at the prospect that awaited them.

"It's about a mile? It's a nice day? We've still a little time?" Suzie said brightening up remarkably from her previous funk. She found her suggestions being met with nothing but blank faces from the other two. "I'm walking." Suzie said strolling off when she saw no takers.

Suzie started across the main road and decided to take a bit of a loop down the streets Mersey Road and Stokesay Road, for no reason other than that detour particularly appealed. Pausing on these streets she reached the conclusion no greatness ever came from places such as these. Finally she reached the Village at the same time as the others, rendezvousing in the car park as planned tacitly, truth be told it was a complete fluke they all ended up in the same place together as they really didn't plan the trip well at all.

"How was the taxi?" Suzie asked smiling at Luci.

"Pricey. The bus, Alex?" Luci questioned.

"Don't ask" Alex said wincing. After the high calibre interchange, the three became aware of a noise coming from the corner of the carpark. They span to see Zed in the corner of the carpark sat in in the cockpit of his ship making 'brrmm, brrmm' noises and looking really happy.

"I'm going to kill him. Elaborately" was all Luci could muster.

Chapter 5 – Alive in the Super Oh Too well known

In a decent sized chamber on a large spaceship Helena and Jane sit opposite each other, a small table with a few lifestyle magazines strewn across the separation between them. They stare silently at each other, all avenues of conversation dried up after months in deep space. The ability to feign even vague interest in each other dissipated. Ennui seeping out of them like a person having drunk ten pints of water whilst camping in a sleeping bag with a bust zip.

Some penny in Jane's brain drops like the push penny machine in an arcade after £18.49 in coppers had been entered into it. "Majesty we're on."

"What do you mean?" Helena asked disinterested.

"I don't know really" Jane stated, "I've just had this kind of protagonist, antagonist, protagonist, antagonist feel of late, whatever that means." Jane stared up "I can't really explain it, but I feel we should be doing *something*.".

"I don't know what you're talking about, I assume its cabin fever, but that's OK." Helena said surprisingly charitably.

"We should make the most of this time together, we have the time and brains to create anything we want really! The world is our playground" Jane said enthusiastically.

"I've got nothing" Helena stated "Maybe I could get a lacky to put on a wash load…" her voice drifted off as she patted her spangly jacket pockets for signs of gin bottles, a dread in her stomach confirming she was out.

"Weeeellll,,," Jane started coyly "I have a rap that I've been working on…now seems like as good a time as any to perform it."

"FOR THE LOVE OF GOD NO!!!" Helena began, but too late, Jane started making a noise that was either an attempt at beat box or some elaborate and music-less form of heart attack. Jane stood up for full effect and started to hop from side to side in what may be the most unco-ordinated piece of dancing since, The Firthonians from the Planet Multi Left Feet attempted to do low gravity Riverdance.

"My name is Jane and I bring the pane…Windows, like a computer platform…No high heel shoes, I take no bull from the headmasters cane…" Helena tried to shut the sound out and started repeatedly hitting herself over the head with a rolled up copy of the Radio Times (it must have been around Christmas time in that part of space) in the hope with enough blows she could reach unconsciousness.

At this point the tale moves from these two figures as plans were afoot, possibly ahand, elsewhere. But mostly as the rap was bad. Really bad.

In space no one can hear you scream, but they can hear you rap. Alas.

Chapter here and now – A thin cut spud atop the scapula

Suzie could swear the air was getting thicker. And greasier. They moved along the rows of shops lining the side of the village before the neon sign of the Seaway came into view on their right. As they neared the door smoke seemed to billow out forming the words "turn back before it's too late" and "it'll rot your guts" and finally "hello mum!" the smoke even managed to get the punctuation mark in. Impressive.

Luci looked at the others and gave a signal that said 'I got this one'. Paying no heed to the smoke based warnings she stepped across the threshold the oily fried smell burning deep into her lungs. She closed the gap from the door to counter in a heartbeat, opening her mouth to speak. Before she could get any words out, the toothless crone tending to the (food may be a stretch of a descriptor here) *items* in the fryer span to give Luci a Blackpool Rock hard stare. "No chips!" she bellowed at Luci.

"Now look here…" Luci began adopting the drunken WC Fields defensive stance ready to take this encounter to the end.

"No Chips!!" the bulky woman repeated in a way that broached no argument. Sheepishly, Luci the most powerful assassin in the eight parts of the known universe to three parts of the unknown universe ratio, backed off beaten. She retreated to the doorway head bowed, with a curtsey thrown in to be on the safe side, where the others were loitering, and thus depriving a few scallies of their usual spot to hang out.

"What happened?" Suzie asked a note of concern in her voice.

"She...she's just too powerful for me..." Luci responded, her body hunched, staring at the ground, Suzie gave Luci an encouraging rub on her back.

"Leave this to thee thy good fellows!" Zed said drawing himself to his full height (about five foot four on a good day, three foot six if he was having a height 'mare), before slumping a little as it felt like the right height for the circumstances. He strolled up to the counter, he possible added a bit of a saunter into his journey, as it was just the way the day was going. He cleared his throat and prepared to put on his best (or best fitting) diction.

"No chips!" the guardian of the fried beige stuff yelled getting in their pre-emptive strike.

"Now listen here m'lady (I thinketh...?)" Zed started undeterred "I have a valuableth quest and must find the clue hidden by the Quizzicals and trusted to your considerable presence to defend." The creature eyed Zed with curiosity and more than a hint of playful malice. She considered repeating her absence of sliced fried potato-based mantra but thought better of it. She spun on the spot and approached the smoking fryer behind her, she instantly plunged her hand within. Without flinching she produced a chip from the burning liquid, though its relationship to a potato bore all the similarity of resemblance of a chimp to a shark in a tuxedo.

She placed the faint yellow and bright green scrap on the counter in front of Zed and looked at him intently. Zed followed the look all too well and what was expected of him now. He picked up the digit, grease instantly running down his fingers which would cause pain to most mortals, but Zed was too stupid to observe such tradition. He placed the thing in his mouth. He chewed, it tasted pretty good actually, probably needed salt, and swallowed opening his mouth to the guardian to show all traces gone. The creature met his eyes and their gaze locked for a minute, possibly two, three absolute tops. She leaned over the counter to look at Zed's stomach region then a little lower. Seeing no seepage or explosions a look of satisfied formality (whatever that is) crept over her face.

"No Chips!" she declared and pointed to the newspapers on the counter. Zed peered closer and saw the top paper was running the headline 'Your next clue beardy!'. Zed snatched up the paper and hurried back to his companions.

"Beholdeth the next clue!" he declared triumphantly, the other three cheered and patted him on the back for his heroism.

Alex began to read from the paper "Jasmine from Bradford who enjoys playing scrabble and badger baiting…" their eyes suddenly darting to the photo that accompanied the article.

Zed snatched the paper "Wrong way around, sorry Liege!", flipping it around disguising what sounded like a disappointed 'ooh' from Alex.

"OK." Suzie began, clearing her throat then clearing her mind. Finally, she cleared her nose and bowels to be on the safe side.

*"'There was a man from Nantucket
Who bought himself a pig
With the express intention of…sorry you want a clue, the clue is below'"*

Suzie looked confused at this elaborate preamble to the clue proper, but read on:

*"'If you want to cross between a ridge
Add a 'B' to the last word in the line above
Use me to cross rivers too
I'm quite near and in me you can drink beer until blue'"*

"The Bridge!" Luci, Zed and Suzie yelled in unison, Zed might have said "Thy Bridge", or something equally stupid.

"Err, yeah, beat me to it." Alex said cowishly to give the sheep a break. After a pause, or hooves, the three continued to stare at Alex.

Zed took pity, "M'ludy, is there a pub called The Bridge in the vicinity of Planet Earth?"

"Oh yeah its near Sale town centre back where we started" there was a collective groan and Luci seemed to punch herself in the jaw. The three left the doorway the smell of grease escaping their nostrils and ear canals, each step making them feel lighter and slightly less clogged up in the arteries.

Immediately on exit a silver bolt from above struck the car parked outside the chip shop, flattening the vehicle (looked like it might once have been a Renault Clio) into scraps. The bolt drew itself up revealing itself to be some kind of gleaming cyborg type thing "Oi you can't park there tinny!" the voice of the resident yelled from a flat above the shops. The silver creature ignored this instruction and fixed on the four heroes, its internal processor confirming these were the targets due for termination with extreme prejudice and opened its mouth to speak.

"Radical!" it declared and flexed its piledriver like arms stepping towards our heroes menacingly.

Chapter on this page - (near enough) Half Time Analysis

Gary of the sports mad alien race The Wordcountupians turned to face his studio companions who were stood around a four dimensional holo-sphere (which seemed a dimension or two more than was necessary for some of the characters) which had been playing the action of the quest out. "Well, what do you make of that Edem? I think half time may just have come at the right time for our heroes who looked to me like they were beginning to flag?"

"Well Gary" Began Edem, a slimy orange alien dressed uncomfortably in a blue blazer, club tie[69] and some bright yellow shell suit bottoms "the gang have got a couple of clues so far and that's good, but for me, the lad Zed will be disappointed with his performance so far, he's got better technique with his movement than he's used so far. Still at the end of the day, it will be the team that finds all the clues first that gets to the glove that wins the match and they will be over the moon with that." Edem folded his arms. He was famed for the immaculate insight, stating the somethin' obvious summary skills and for the all smelling eye that sat in the middle of his ridged forehead.

"And Maya" Gary turned to the second pundit, who was meticulously dressed in a plaid suit and had a large data slate in one hand with a

---

[69] Mint club by the looks of it.

satchel containing reams of detailed notes she had made as part of her research over her shoulder, "what do you make of this new character the T10001 that's turned up? He looks like an exciting acquisition for Queen Helena's team, if she could just find the right formation to fit him in? I'm not sure the current role brings out the best of his...its, ability but, with the right support act, sparks could literally fly with him? Maybe if she added him to a part flat pack back pack four? What do you think?"

Maya considered the question made a few mental notes in her head (which housed a brain so large and powerful that a large fork lift truck was required to support her cranium in the studio) and took a deep breath, ready to impart the wisdom of the ages for the studio to understand the mechanics of the universe at play. Well..."

"...Exactly!" Gary agreed eagerly. "Edem, what do you think Helena will be saying to her troops at half time?"

After a few minutes distractedly looking into the holo-sphere, Edem broke his gaze from it and turned to Gary "Well Gary. I think she is going to want to keep it tight again. The scientists have reluctantly played their part but with this T101 Robert they've created they've definitely helped her get a foothold in the quest. Now if the elite troops can just lump it up to the big man; Jane and chuck a few more general direction plots into the mixer then they could have this wrapped up early doors." Edem went to lean back in his chair a little satisfied, then after momentarily panicking and flailing corrected himself as he realised he was stood up.

Gary smiled and nodded encouragingly at Edem. He hadn't a clue what he was talking about, but he was popular with viewers. "Maya, the chip shop part of the story. Do you think that held up as to scrutiny as the right place to house a clue?"

Maya smiled at Gary "My thinking formed from millennia of study and research is that…"

"…I couldn't agree more." Gary stated "I think the audience watching, I mean reading, at home would be in total agreement with you there as well." Gary turned back to Edem "And which of our heroes do you think will be most happy with how they've performed in this adventure so far?"

Edem mopped his brow around his third eye, the studio lights didn't agree with him and he was secreting more slime than ever, bourn out by the camera man who had slid across the studio on the background. "Well I think Luci has got to be proud of the army of giant snails she has sent into the fray, the opposition were not expecting that when…"

"…Sorry Edem I'll have to stop you on that one" Gary twitched nervously, "that's not happened yet, but who knows the way this quest is going it may well be imminent." He turned once more to Maya "So given your vast understanding of the cosmos, how do you think the world is going to turn out?"

Maya nodded politely at the question, she had been waiting for this. She didn't especially enjoy sport, but she thought if she could get herself a decent media and public profile through it, she would be able to impart the wisdom of the universe on the public subconsciously, make them see the error of their disposable consumer culture ways, then surely that was a start towards a kinder, loving, more collaborative, considerate world. "It's quite straightforward the universe when you think about its Gary. What it all boils down to is..."

"...Maya, sorry I'm going to have to stop you there, we have Tony the Cherubim who has an interview with the chip shop crone we've just seen in action. Tony over to you"

"Gary, thank you." Tony was flying around the head of the chip shop guardian holding a microphone out to her "And how do you feel you played your part in the adventure as it has unfolded?" The crone contemplated, tossing the question around in her head, considering all the permutations.

"No Chips!" she bellowed.

"Thanks for the insight, good luck with the rest of your adventure" Tony declared happily shaking the creature by the hand before she walked off. "Gary back to you in the studio".

"Thanks for that Tony." Gary again returned his gaze to Maya. "So, we were discussing the possibilities of the universe and you had some insight to impart Maya?" Maya smiled sweetly once more and opened her mouth to speak "…And I'll have to stop you there as we go to a commercial break. Don't go away"

Chapter iiiviixiixiillmmm© - There is a chip shop in England that absolutely does not sell chips and no one in there thinks they're Elvis (although one person went to a Stars in Their Eyes talent show as The Human League[70])

"Sorry to bum you out dudes and dudettes, but you've got to die, orders of the most bodacious Queen Helena of planet Eccles!" a metallic voice rang out through the village. The residents looked non plussed at best, they preferred their murder robots more sports casual.

Suzie flinched "Does that mean what I think it does?"

"Certainly m'lady, 'that' is a very specific sword used to identify a specific person or thing observed or heard by the speaker. Or so the ye olde dictionary tells me". Zed tried to be helpful.

"You're an idiot." Suzie said plainly to Zed.

"Less academia, more asskickademia!" Roared Luci (who was not very good at puns, less so battle cries). She preceded to perform a full double somersault to land in front of the robot, as quick as a flash (other bathroom cleaners are available) she performed 'The Moe', a move of deadly grace and precision involving

---

[70] They came third behind Tina from Pontefract who did a salsa infused version of 'Plague Rages' by Napalm Death and Barry from Hull who did a fantastic version of The London Philharmonic Orchestra performing Tchaikovsky's 1812 Overture

sticking your fingers in the eyes of your assailant.

Luci took a half step back perturbed as the fingers just bounced off the reinforced lenses of the automaton. Luci flipped back away from the robot's rapid counter punch. The machine paused, unhappy with the fingerprint smudges on its lenses, it took a silk handkerchief with comedy pigs from its pocket (they said to the T10001's creator that a robot doesn't need pockets, but who is laughing now? Oh no one…) and wiped its ocular devices, before checking the handkerchief to see what magic the contents revealed. The robot took another step forward.

"I think verily thy have this machine all wrong" Zed piped up "He's a large robot, he's a long way from home, he's in Ashton Village, we just gotta get him a pint of oil and he's ok!" Zed started to approach the machine, before anyone could say 'Zed you pillock, that's a highly advanced killing machine which has been sent to Earth with the express orders of hurting us all really badly' (admittedly for a warning they should have picked a more pithy turn of phrase). The machine met Zed with a backhand swipe sending him flying through the air hitting a car with a heavy 'thud' (might have been a 'bong').

"Oi watch the car!" shouted a resident from outside the fight.

"Zed are you OK?" Luci asked genuinely concerned.

"Fine. Happeneth all the time." Zed seemed utterly unphased by what had just happened. Truly he was a professional idiot.

"Bogus!" declared the robot in a way that got Alex thinking. The hamster put its cigarette out, rose from the sofa with a groan, mounted the wheel and slowly started running with a slight limp.

"Suzie's time to shine!" Suzie gave out her not especially intimidating battle cry. She gracefully swiped her top hat off her head and a platoon (squadron? Flotilla? Herd? Murder?) of doves flew out pooing on the robot on their way out and past. "Take that tin head!" Suzie declared with a triumphant giggle.

"And that's achieved?" Luci asked.

"That stuff is a nightmare to get off, he's gonna have serious rust problems in a few years!" Suzie clarified.

"Bummer!" the machine mused.

"Anything a little more, you know, immediate?" Luci asked impatiently.

"Err…"

"I've got it!" Alex declared. The hamster satisfied with its work and knackered after reaching speeds of up to four RPMs got off the wheel, eased itself gingerly back onto the sofa and lit another cigarette. "Anyone got a USB lead?", looking at the blank faces that met him, Alex realised they'd have to source one themselves "distract him. It. Whatever!" Suzie saw the cue and removed her hat again, drew three canes throwing one each to Zed and Luci. She then threw the hat to Zed and the three of them started an elaborate, yet spontaneous, Busby Berkley type dance routine. Given the impromptu nature of this show, it was surprisingly impressive, it had high kicks and everything.

Alex ducked their head back into the chip shop "do you have a USB lead? It's a matter of life and..."

"...No chips!" The crone shouted unfastening the studio microphone from her lapel.

"Ah of course." Alex was not to be defeated and after literally minutes of looking around the village somehow found a USB lead. Let's say a passing winged monkey passed Alex the USB lead for the sake of completeness. It might be what happened, it was a fast-moving fluid battle situation after all.

Alex tentatively approached the machine which was appreciatively tapping its foot along to the dance routine. Getting close enough Alex plugged in the USB into the conveniently prominent front slot on the machine. The automaton turned its gaze menacingly to Alex and weighed up the most interesting options in its programmes to pulp this human upstart. Alex knew they had one shot at this, they flicked through the film library on their phone. The machine raised its arms, servos whirring, building up to 'insta-death' speed. Finding what they were looking for Alex pressed play. The machine swung its arm at murderous velocity, millimetres from Alex's face it stopped, opened its palm and patted Alex's head.

"Awesome!" the robot declared, somehow managing to sound happy, despite its programming only containing the emotions anger, hatred, grumpy anger, rage, ire and to mix things up a little sangfroid.

Seeing their work done, Alex turned to the others "Guys! Guys?!"

"Wait, wait we're building up to the big finish!" Suzie said impatiently. And with that Zed leapt surprisingly gracefully in the air to be caught by the two women with a collective "ta da!". Alex found themselves applauding involuntarily.

Luci gently lowered Zed to the ground on his head. "Oh yeah!" she declared suddenly pulling the horn she kept in her belt and blowing hard on it. The horn made a sound that sounded suspiciously like the theme music to the TV show Minder. There was a pause. Then nothing. Nothing happened.

"Oh" said Luci disappointedly.

"What was that m'lady?" Zed asked picking himself off the ground head last.

"In my moment of direst need, if I blow on that horn, salvation will arrive." Luci clarified with a hint of pride.

"But you can see the robot is no threat, I've pacified it. We didn't need any help. Haven't you kind of wasted it?" Alex asked.

"I panicked!" Luci said sheepishly.

"Well what happens?" Suzie asked.

"Well err…you see…there is this…well when things are bad then…I don't know." Luci admitted. They waited a few minutes longer. Nothing happened. Again.

"Come on let's go." Suzie decided, turning to Alex "How did you know to stop that thing?" she asked.

"Simple really. I recognised the early 90s surfer speech pattern. I've plugged it into Point Break, seems it was all he needed."

"He needs to broaden his film palette." Luci muttered.

Chapter XXX (a steamy or kissy chapter?) – Fly you fowls

"So, we walk back to Sale, to this place, The Bridge yeah?" Suzie asked sheltering from the sudden shower under the Co-Op overhang (lots of Co-Ops in Sale. And undesirables, lots of them too).

"Not so fast thy good lady!" Zed countered "we have the puritunnelical!" With that Zed crossed his arms across his chest in a way that suggested the words he had just used provided exactly all the explanation that was necessary.

"I'm going to regret this…" Alex started "…but what in the name of armchair sports is that?!"

"Aha! Verily straightforward!" Zed declared triumphantly "The youngsters, the elders having been voted out on an online poll that, they couldn't understand how to register for, anyway I digressteth, the youngsters to aid me on this nobleth quest, gave me this scroll to aid our glory. It opens a gateway between locations in the quickest and purest meaneth available. Whatever all that means. Verily." Zed smiled at all his companions unable to work out why they were looking at his with utter suspicion at best.

"Oh no." Alex said firmly "I'm not doing any of that magic travel stuff, I've seen The Fly, both versions. Never ends well. I'm walking. See you there." And with that Alex started to move off pulling their collar up to shelter from the current hard falling rain.

"Well I've a feeling that given what happened with your ship I should set my expectations low but show us what you got!" Luci encouraged Zed, she'd had enough tedium for the day and was in the mood for some magic to take the edge of the dullness that was creeping in. Suzie seeing Luci was willing to take the risk nodded, her top hat coming off her head so vigorous was her agreement.

Zed reached into a pocket hidden deep in his cape, drew out a mini pork pie and took a large bite accidently biting his fingers in the process. He placed the pork pie back in his 'save for later' pocket. He then produced his mobile phone and scrolled to the pdf saver where he had downloaded all his sacred e-parchments.

"Ah ghh hem agh!" Zed began. After satisfactorily clearing his throat he pressed play on his phone. 'Crockett's Theme' from Miami Vice by Jan Hammer started playing as a green swirling smoke began to pour forward from Zed's phone, it formed some kind of swirling tunnel. "Just let me type in the postcode of thy destination." Zed said whilst typing on his phone "and thee just walk through it and verily we'll be at thou destination.". With that, Zed stepped forward into the smoke which part enveloped him leaving a ghostly trace of his idiot shell. Suzie saw Zed move in there seemingly unharmed and after a pause to take a deep breath stepped in after him.

Luci entered behind the other two staring around in awe at the strobing beauty on the inside of the tunnel giving her a sense of weightlessness "bloody hell it's pretty!" she declared enchanted. At this point one of the swirling smoke tendrils formed into an open hand and slapped her across the face. "What the bloody heck!" Luci yelled and the hand slapped her in the face again. "Zed! What the bugger is this?!" Another slap.

"Ah well you see the puritunnelical was designedeth by the elders as a last act to try and A. get the youngsters to school on time and B. to stop them misbehaving. It doesn't take well to violence, swearing or sexeth. It mighteth be why the youngsters were so happy to give it to me" Zed explained matter of factly.

"No bloody chance of the last thing!" Suzie muttered receiving a slap for her troubles.

"Zed you idiot!" Luci shouted and received a slap in reply "How is idiot swearing?!" she howled into the tunnel, prompting another slap.

"For f…" Suzie began, getting a slap for her troubles "Flip, I was going to say flip!" the hand sprung back out and rubbed Suzie's face by way of apology.

At this point after what seemed like an eternity, but was actually a matter of minutes[71] and after many threats and actual carrying out threats of violence, combined with swearing at Zed and a

---

[71] As Anyone who has heard Sweet Caroline at a wedding (and if you've been to a wedding, you've heard Sweet Caroline) can attest to, a matter of minutes can feel like a lifetime.

hefty dose of slaps all-round the three character emerged from the end of the swirling fog tunnel, their arms up trying to protect their face, to see Alex on the other side of the street doubled up with laughter.

"You saw all that?" Luci asked with more than a hint of miff in her voice, as she rubbed her face to try and sooth the sting.

"Every step and slap" Alex confirmed still creased up "it was piss funny" At this point a hand stretched out of the fog and gave them a slap. "Aww."

Suzie took in her new surroundings "We've gained five metres from that fu...fog!" she wailed "how is that possible?!"

"Err…the youngsters weren't very good with co-ordinates it seemseth." Zed said brightly unphased by the last few minutes.

Luci clenched her fist looked at Zed, looked at the fog swirling over her shoulder, looked back at Zed and thought better of it. For now.

"Walk?" Alex asked. The others nodded painfully in agreement. "Tell me Zed" Alex began "did the elders ever watch an Earthen film called The Blues Brothers…"

Chapter D – Sitting in a tin can dock of the bay

Due to the time spent whiling away in the vastness of space, Helena had taken to painting as a hobby. She had created a challenging (her words) series called 'dull things I see out of the window'. This was a series of black canvass pictures with white stars added in Tipex (which Helena was prone to a quick swig of, to 'encourage' the creative juices[72]). Jane hadn't had the heart yet to tell Helena she was failing to capture the sweeping majesty of the universe. Or to capture even the accurately of applying Tipex to black canvas.

Jane approached Helena with care, having no idea how to break the bad news she had. She toyed with putting it between some jokes (and she had a couple of cracking jokes about vanilla blancmange up her sleeve), or hiding the news in Helena's pudding, like some kind of disappointing tuppence. In the end she felt nothing for it but, a full-frontal assault, both barrels, hit her with the truth between the eyes.

"Majesty, you are looking splendid this afternoon..." she quickly checked her watch "...evening and what a beautiful space evening it is too. Can I get you a gin. Maybe a kebab to go with it?"

---

[72] Don't try this at home kids. Especially if in deep space, if you happen to live there.

"What happened?" Helena interrupted in a neutral voice.

"Well, you see, its that robot chap, we've lost contact." Jane said involuntarily flinching.

"Lost contact? He's chipped isn't he?" Helena enquired.

"True mighty queenie. He's on the map, he appears to be stationary in a place called Ashton On Mersey. His neurocircuits are on a two hour and two-minute loop spiking away. Somethings got to him" Jane stated.

Helena paused from her painting "And you've tried to contact him?" her eyebrow shooting to the sky.

"Yes, we've had contact, we had to get our finest dude translators on it. He keeps saying mystic surf types things, they think they've narrowed it down to, but they still can't ascertain the meaning of any of it. It seems to be nonsense masquerading as something profound" Jane said not entirely confident in (m)any of the words she had just used.

"Oh."

"But also, I bring good news…" Jane hoped this may improve the atmosphere, although right now a stout and broccoli vindaloo fart would have improved the atmosphere.

"…Let me guess, some previously forgotten about army that we can get to Earth lickety spit?" Helena interrupted.

Jane was taken aback, to about three weeks ago by her reckoning. It was a nice place to go back and spend a short holiday in. "Err, yeah exactly that. The elite blue flat caps are just around the corner from Earth, they were on some kind of reconnaissance mission, which they say that not at liberty to reveal any of the details about to me. I'll give them a phone call and ask if they mind popping down and doing some roughing up."

"Good work." Helena decided to offer a little praise for once. "Let me show you my latest picture, I'm calling it 'Black with Mr Speckly White making a cheeky appearance' come have a long look and drink it all in".

Jane felt her stomach lurch.

Meanwhile uptown a DJ play. And by 'Uptown' that would be the planet Generic Space Name, Zargoden or Something (The discover of this planet was notoriously weak when it came to naming their discoveries with any conviction)

Heimrich was depressed. He'd been playing the same nightclub on (lets shorten it to) Zargoden for years. It should be the easiest most fun gig in the solar system. The people of Zargoden were relentlessly upbeat to the point of being smugly overbearing and they loved to dance, oh how they loved to dance. They'd been known to hit speeds of Mach two when there were rumours of a break-dancing competition in town. They consequently needed no excuse to whip their T-shirts off (which is quite a lot of admin when you have eight arms) and throw their arms in the air. Sometimes even taking the time to catch them on the way back down.

However, Heimrich was still down. Playing tracks such as 'Isn't the World Wonderful?', 'Throw your hands in the air and shout woo hoo!' and 'let's dance forever as nothing bad will ever happen to us!' (none of which were ironic titles) just filled him with, well filled him with nothing. They were meaningless platitudes that failed to acknowledge the full spectrum, or even a chunk of the spectrum, of emotion and feeling. Playing endless upbeat numbers to a load of eight armed hedonists all seemed like shooting fish in a barrel to Heimrich and brought him no satisfaction.

Sure, playing these tracks had the dancefloor punching their arms in the air (and where a congregation of people with eight arms throw them in the air simultaneously, you best hold onto something lest the draft created knocks you off your feet), but it felt hollow to Heimrich, like people weren't truly feeling what power music could fully have over them. Heimrich considered himself superior as he 'felt' music and liked it to challenge him, even though it made him miserable and an unbearable snob, he felt he had an authenticity others couldn't match. Basically, Heimrich was a pillock.

Whilst queuing up the next generic ode to the world being a wonderful place for dancing in, Heimrich noted a hulking bouncer turning away a local at the door. Too casual seemed to be the reason, on account of a bangle on one of the eight wrists. Considering their upbeat nature, Zargodian door policies could be extremely draconian, woe betide anyone who wore trainers to a club (despite it seeming the sensible choice for being on your feet all night dancing).

Tonight, was the night Heimrich was going to give the Zargodians what they really wanted but didn't know it yet. Something powerful, raw, something that would play with their emotions and touch their souls, he reasoned with more than a hint of over self-importance. They just weren't aware it was missing in their life yet, but once exposed to it, it would give them a yearning for more, a thirst that would never be sated. That's why people go for nights out in cheap social clubs Heimrich felt.

He'd been shopping in the 'Hyper-Word Music' section of the record shop and had found some gems from an unremarkable planet called Earth. He was going to give them both barrels 'Disorder' by Joy Division, 'Grey Geisha' by Tim Hecker and Daniel Lopatin, 'Monsters Theme' by Jon Hopkins and most of all 'An Ending' by Brian Eno. Heimrich queued all the records up in turn and let them play. As the melodies flowed, Heimrich felt the music course through his Bacardi encrusted veins, sparking thoughts and feelings he couldn't explain and if he even tried to, the spell would be broken.

And yet, nothing. For all the education Heimrich felt he was giving them, the Zargodians looked unimpressed, edgy for something they'd heard at least a couple of hundred times before. Given the Zargodians survived the Great Crisp Drought of 2421 with a smile on their faces and a shrug in their shoulders, the expressions he was seeing on the faces in front of him struck Heimrich as odd.

Heimrich ploughed on, scratching over the records, beat mixing three records at once, punching the air with 2 arms and picking his nose, he glanced over the decks and could see Az the Bar Owner's (his actual surname, apostrophe and everything) face which said 'play them something they know and definitely like. Preferably something upbeat' (Az having a very expressive face where choice of record was concerned), although its equally possible his facial expression might have been 'I think I left a cheese and onion pie in the oven on the wrong gas mark at home', Heimrich wasn't sure. Either way, Heimrich knew he had to switch it up, rescue the situation, be the hero 'nothing for it' he thought as he queued up 'I hate myself and I want to Die' by Nirvana.

Chapter imminent – Abridged Script of the Bridge

Our heroes (perhaps heroes is too stronger term? The heroics have been kept to a bare minimum so far. A more accurate collective is required, Gobshites? Eejits? Numbskulls? Omnishambles? Burks?).

Our eejits (will do for now) found themselves at the edge of the car park staring at the pub The Bridge. It being a glorious day in Manchester (and by that, the sun occasionally poked its head out from a sheet of grey, before deciding better of what was happening below and scampering off for a duvet day. The temperatures were reaching a dog in the car non-threatening fifteen degrees with high likelihood of constant showers). Due to these factors the outdoor section was teeming with drunken people, wearing very little, working the 'I feel no sunburn now, that is tomorrow's problem, in the meantime – here is to alcohol!' look.

The four intelligence challenged companions walked through the car park reaching the steps leading to the unknown pleasures above. On the surface, the patio area had a pleasant vibe, if you could look past the parents shouting obscenities at their kids and the bloke violently throwing up over the wall onto the cyclists on the canal tow path below. The four ascended the steps.

"Question." Alex started.

"You forgot the question mark in your punctuation ergo it's not a question." Came back Luci.

"How could you see what punctuation I…look never mind. What exactly are we looking for?" Alex asked as a drunken shape barged though them despite the considerable space to either side for them to pass.

"Well, thy honour, since this was set by the quizzicals…" Zed began to make a case.

"…The flippin' obvious!" Luci butted in saving them all a lot of time and nonsense words. "Split up again. Anyone other than Zed check the bar"

"No need." Suzie sighed cocking her head (but deciding against pulling the trigger). Following her directions, except Zed who was distracted by the specials menu, the group saw an elderly lady with bright eyes and a wide goofy smile, who was reading an oversized book entitled 'Looking for a clue that will help you find that gauntlet thingy that will save, or destroy, the world? Then you've come to the right place mister (or Ms)'. In retrospect the book had to be that large to fit the title in. They tentatively stepped towards the lady unsure how to start the conversation.

"Hello my dears!" the lady said warmly as she saw them approaching "You're looking to save the world, or ruin it into some kind of not very pleasant oppression yes?" before anyone could respond "What can I get you to drink?"

"Oh no its…" Suzie started.

"…Four pints of scrumpieth!" Zed cut across. "Anyone else but thy want a drink?" he stepped excitedly from side to side at the prospect.

With that the lady skipped from her seat, made her way past the four and entered the bar. The three spun and stared at Zed who seemed not to notice them glaring at him despite every face being millimetres from his. It was quite the group shot.

Presently (pastly being out of date) the lady returned from the bar holding four pints and what looked like a glass of incredibly strong ale impressively in her hands. She sat down and produced two chasers, no one had the courage to ask how she had transported those.

"May I ask?" Suzie asked anyway.

"Yes dearie?" the lady fixed her with a smile.

"Well Mrs…" Suzie began tentatively

"Betty, call me Betty love."

"Betty? That's a nice name" Suzie said kindly.

"It's not my real name, but I feel like a Betty today." Betty (as established) beamed.

"Do you wait here all day, waiting to give out a clue, on the off chance someone might turn up needing it?" Suzie asked.

"Yes, pretty much. It's nice enough, the people are friendly really and I find out all the gossip." She gave the party on over-elaborate wink.

"You should hear what Carol at number fifty-four Waverley Road is up to. The foxy lady. I mean actual foxes..." She leaned back chuckling, "...come sit down with me" she gestured at the spare chairs. The four took seats.

"Oh ok. But, drinking all day, that must take its toll?" Suzie asked with a hint of genuine concern.

"Oh no." Betty chuckled "This is just shandy" She nodded at her beer "And those are just apple juice" She now pointed at the shots. "Old TV trick." She took a sip of the pint "Drinking all day is a dangerous path leading to a dark lonely place. Besides, I'm on duty." She laughed again.

"I've a question now" Began Alex "You give the clue to anyone who asks?"

"Oh yes, I'm happy to help." Betty confirmed with a vigorous nod.

"But there are those that would seek the gauntlet to use it for means of ill, I mean doing really ill things." Alex stated with genuine concern.

"Ah you see." Betty took another swig "How do you know and define their intention? A person's motive is a question of perspective and often their goal is bound in complexities that are not easily boiled down to good and bad, few things are. Many who gain the power they seek often find it wasn't the solution they anticipated and those that misuse find themselves soon enough in a stark and isolated place. Since the dawn of this planet, and indeed the universe, people have sought control of others and committed atrocities. They would argue purpose in and justification of their acts, despite all evidence to the contrary. And yet, and yet, humanity always seems to find small and large ways to prevail, there are always good people doing good things and that hope is to be clung on to. This planet still turns for now, though there are plenty of pillocks, if you will mind my language, doing their best to stop that, but hopefully there will always be decent people challenging said pillocks, if you will pardon my language a second time. So, I give whoever asks their clue and let them figure the route they take themselves knowing that there will always be some kindness somewhere which cannot be quenched. Its been OK as a tactic so far. Sorry I've rambled on and not really answered your question there have ?" She laughed heartily.

The four sat momentarily stunned, though in Zed's case it had lasted longer than momentarily, it could have been the scrumpy he just necked, or just his general lack of gorm. Betty took a sip of her apple juice this time. "I know what you're thinking, I'm that classic trope of that twinkly eyed old lady turning out homespun wisdom. Well I am in this guise, but it seems to work." She placed her glass down. "Would anyone like a biscuit?"

From seemingly nowhere, Betty proffered a surprisingly neat plate of biscuits including the lesser spotted Foxys party rings, and there wasn't even a party going on. A couple of the group accepted; Zed and Alex.

"Anyway" Betty continued "You'll be wanting your clue?" The four nodded in surprisingly well choreographed unison. "OK here I go, I apologise up front for the low-grade quality of the clue. Those quizzicals, bless 'em, aren't quite as smart as they imagine, and nominative determinism hasn't really worked for them." She cleared her throat.

"Friends, Romans, countrymen
Lend me your socks
The next clue is in Sale Tesco
Ask for Alan at the sub cheese counter."

"I'll be honest, I think the Quizzicals were running out of ideas." Betty chortled "rhymes too it seems, I wouldn't mind, but plenty rhymes with socks, but let's not ponder that too much".

"I think that all mistakenly implies they had ideas to run out of…" Luci muttered to herself.

"Would you like to stay for another drink? It's a pretty nice day, for Manchester" Betty asked pleasantly.

Showing the reflexes of the finely honed assassin she was, Luci replied (only just) before Zed could commit to more drinks. "No, we really must go and complete our quest, the hour is very nearly upon us. But thanks."

The four stood up on that cue. "Oh, and Alex?" Betty said evenly.

Alex stopped dumbfounded "How did you know my name?"

"Doesn't matter dear, again it goes with the territory of this trope." She fixed him with a broad goofy smile "it'll be OK. In the end its all OK. Honest." Alex found these words comforting and involuntarily smiled back matching Betty and nodded.

Suddenly a megaphone boomed (or it might have bipped) "You four idiots!" The four companions looked around to see who this voice was addressing "No the four of you not drunk and looking around!". This time the companions did a quick totting up to confirm their numbers. "That's right, you, the ones dressed like the pan galactic Village People."

"Now that's just a dated reference." muttered Alex.

"You are to surrender. Now!" The voice boomed further. More booming than a convention of mobile TV microphone operators seemed to be happening in the car park at this time.

Our collective name of characters turned now (something they might have considered to have been beneficial doing earlier) to see a Platoon (battalion, squad, flotilla, legion, posse, gang, duo? Naming these collectives isn't easy) of Helena's troops massed in the pub car park armed to the teeth (dental weaponry being all the rage in the Eccles space belt) "For you the quest is over." Stated Captain Megaphone Operator (an assumed name) lowering the megaphone down to her thigh. Captain Megaphone Operator turned to the waiting troops behind her and said in a voice that sounded exactly the same (pitch, volume and even static feedback) as when she was using the megaphone "take them!".

Chapter – First of the Winter Moonshine

Odin sat on the office swivel chair nervously turning one way and then another. He involuntarily kept playing with his tie, twirling it in his fingers, it was itchy and he knew it didn't suit him, but it was the self-appointed[73] Rulers of the Universe, AKA The Immortals[74], AKA the busy body gits fortnightly meeting.

He took another tentative sip of his dust flavoured supermarket cheapest brand tea and contemplated if dunking a rich tea biscuit in it would make it taste any better, he figured not, as this brew was beyond redemption of a mere mortal biscuit.

"OK, so the speed bumps on the star belt into Acuna" began Thea, who had drawn the short straw and was chairing the meeting again. Thea hated chairing the meeting, as it meant she had to actually pay attention to what other people were saying. What she really wanted to do was sit at the back of the room and keep her head down doodling. And when you have twenty-five and a half tentacles like Thea did, you could do some impressive doodles. Her smiley faces were amazing. "Zach have you actioned them? Zach…Zach!"

"Huh?" Zach snorted in a half woken state and said something that sounded suspiciously like

---

[73] Never trust anything self-appointed

[74] Debate rages about whether the Immortals are called such as they live forever, or as they have the ability to last through the regular meetings.

"I'll take you all on!" raising his fists and vaguely waving them around in front of his face, before gaining full consciousness "sorry, what was the question? I was busy making detailed notes from the last agenda item." He lied through his forty-foot log teeth; an impressive feat all considered.

"Have you actioned the building of the speedbumps?" Thea said impressively patiently. She wished she'd pulled a sicky before the meeting but being one of a group called The Immortals somewhat exposed the lie of that.

"Have I 'actioned' them?" Zach paraphrased back. "Do you mean have I done them?"

A sound like a hot water pipe springing a large hole and sending torrent of steam out filled the room. Turned out it was Thea sighing. "Yessssss. The speedbumps. Have you *done* them?"

"Yes, I have." Zach confirmed sitting back feeling rather pleased of himself. At this point Odin started to think about what he'd like to have for his tea when he got home. Something with chips to reward himself, he thought as his head suddenly jolted up, realising he'd fallen asleep Odin quickly looked around to see if anyone noticed, on scanning the room everyone was still in the same positions and talking away. Rubbing his chin, the bristles told him he'd been asleep for a couple of days. They appeared to be still be on the agenda item that had immediately followed the speedbumps.

"So, all in favour of that show your hands?" Thea was asking. Odin had no idea what was going on, but this was no exception to most meetings he attended, so he adopted his usual strategy; he put his hand up and voted in favour as fewer disagreements meant maybe the meeting would finish sooner. He remembered that this tactic might once have led to him voting for the unilateral destruction of his sister's home planet; Placemat, but on the plus side, he did get home in time to watch Nebulon 5 Eggheads[75].

"Next item; labelling of sun visors..." Thea was starting. Odin noticed an orange glow emanating from behind the flip chart (so called as anyone disruptive in the meeting was placed on the board and flipped into the nearest uncharted passing vortex) in the corner of the meeting room. Odin raised unsteadily from his seat, most of his limbs having fallen asleep, or at the very least having had a light restorative snooze. Behind the board the glow was brighter still, a luminescent pool that tantalised with visions of possibilities, Odin was pretty confident it was a temporal warp. Conveniently, Odin had read up on these recently. Once entered, the portal could take you to long lost or parallel dimensions, take you to a new place

---

[75] A show where five aliens with actual eggs for heads must combat a team of challengers in a fight to the death with oversized T-spoons.

in time, or equally as likely, atomise your entire body leaving behind a fine sherbet. Odin thought about it for precisely a second, stepping immediately in, reasoning full body disintegration still got him out of the meeting.

Odin's body felt a flush of white heat, half imagined images of people and places he had known, or may one day know, or another version of him had known danced in his eyes. A music that sounded suspiciously like 'Electric Dreams' played through his mind and also through his bowels. He pushed on through the warp, each laboured step meeting more resistance, sending more strange visions firing to his synapses in unexpected directions. The portal was clearing, he was nearly through. One more step. The light faded, Odin took in his new Eden, the new possibility offered by this tear in the fabric of time. He found himself back in the same meeting room albeit ten minutes earlier "Drat!" he cursed managing a not very strong swearword all things considered.

"Sorry." The portal seemed to reply in a surprisingly rich voice. Odin shrugged and took his seat cursing the knitting gods he worshipped.

****

Aeons and a couple of Ice ages later…

"So" Thea started "we're at AOB."

"Any Other Bollocks." Jennifer muttered under her breath, deciding to use the mouth on the back of her dorsal fin lest anyone could lip read.

If Thea had heard this slight, she was applying the time-honoured meeting protocol of ignoring it for now but sending a whole heap of passive aggressive E-Pigeons and unnecessary work the way of the perpetrator over the coming months.

"Well there is this apothecary clove…" Odin began. It was his big moment, that he'd been specifically sent by his advisory council to raise this dire warning. Odin had written the word 'apocalyptic gloves' on his hand to remind him, though this had become a little smudged sweating in the heat of the meeting room.

Unfortunately, Simoon (two Os at the end, no one knew why, much less cared to ask) said, more loudly (easy to do when you're a walking giant pit), "I'm not happy with the risk rating on the intergalactic bank account, I want to revisit this." So after four hours of arguing, it was agreed that the risk colour of the bank running out of paying in slips in the immortals names was 'orange with a dash of crimson and some bule flecks to give it a modern feel', rather than the 'setting sun on the dying husk of a planet red' colour they'd agreed to earlier.

"Any other AOB?" Thea asked with a hint of dread travelling down her spines and totally ignoring the tautology.

"Odin!" Jennifer nudged Odin who had dozed off again. Considering Jennifer was made of rock and plaster of paris this caused Odin considerable ouch. "Didn't you have something?"

"Huh….I'll fight you all…oh yeah. There is this one thing, there is this…err…apoplectic…power…cove…glave…no…glove, or is it gloves, anyway, its thought this glove is able to empower the glove wearer with the power of all the universe's power in the glove, it's called 'the hand warmer of control'. We found it on the Gerlaxon bypass. In the wrong hand the whole universe and all life could be destroyed and…"

"…Where did this glove come from?" Simoon interjected.

"Its origin? I don't know you see…" Odin began.

"…What's it made of? Has it been PAT tested?" came another voice using further tautology with PAT testing.

"I'm not sure that's the point, as…" Odin tried to carry on.

"…Has it been risk rated?" Came another question, probably Simoon.

"It's a glove that can destroy all known life in an instant. I'm risk rating it red. Shitting deep red. Now can we…" Odin spat out, his patience truly gone at this point and Odin wasn't much of a doctor to start with.

163

"...Look you've not come here with enough information, so I suggest we carry this over to the next meeting so Odin can deliver a full PowerPoint presentation on it" Simoon stated.

"No, no that's not necessary" Thea reasoned with one eye on getting this meeting finished and getting to the gym, the other seven eyes she kept on the room. "If this glove is of such power, we must hide it beyond the wit of any mortal. It must be placed in as safe a place as possible and all knowledge of it hidden. The Guardians of this secret must be the bravest, most intelligent, dedicated, single-minded, willing to sacrifice themselves, creatures in the known universe, and maybe we include the unknown parts of the universe, just so we cover that angle again."

"So, who do we give it to?" Jennifer asked.

"Who didn't turn up to the meeting today?" Thea responded.

"The Quizzicals." Replied Simoon.

"Give it to the Quizzicals." Thea confirmed dismisively.

Seeing his role done, or near enough as far as he was concerned, Odin made his excuses to go to the toilet strolling out of the room and as soon as he was out of eyeshot legging it in the nearest direction away from the meeting.

A number of questions still ran through his head as he also ran; 1. Where did that glove come from? 2. How did it end up in a bush on a bypass, had someone treated it like an old school niche interest magazine? 3. Why didn't his leaders just destroy the glove? Were they worried about putting it in the wrong recycle bin? 4. Why do the immortals hold fortnightly meetings? Why does *anyone* hold meetings? 7. Why couldn't Odin count?

****

Meanwhile on planet Quizzical, home of the Quizzicals, believe it or not.

The throne room (the posh toilet) of the principality Quizzical palace was shining in its newly polished resplendent glory. A poorly paid Quizzical intern sat on a stool waiting to administer cheap aftershave and lotions in exchange for copper pennies and toffees.

Steph charged in looking flustered. Turned out she just needed to…make 'a call'. After ablutions were completed, she walked over to the biggest poshest cubicle. She knocked on the door and a voice from within beckoned her in. Steph entered the cubicle, it was a bit of a squeeze with her and supreme leader lady Rhat in it together, but this was the Quizzical protocol. "Lady Rhat, I have the minutes from the last immortals meeting, apologies for the delay but given the size of the attachment I had to delete all my emails to receive the message."

Lady Rhat made a gesture as if waving away these details. She may have been wafting a toilet smell away in hindsight. "What news?" lady Rhat asked. "Did we cop for any actions?"

"All of them, my lady."

"Bollocks" Lady Rhat cursed. "Send them to the work placement Quizzical to deal with as a development opportunity[76]." And with that she yanked hard on the chain.

---

[76] Or as 'Development Opportunities' are better known in the place of work 'shit I don't want to deal with'.

Chapter 4 – Back to Earth with a bump and a knee in the groin

"Oof right in thy danglies!" Zed bent double as a guard stuck a knee fully, and then a little further still, into his groin.

Another guard rubbed his head having foolishly took up Luci's offer to 'hit this hand[77]'. Four of the guards had to run and leapt into the canal (gaining 9.4 on the score cards from the locals for their efforts) as they were chased by a large and slightly manky ferret Suzie had conjured from her hat.

Zed gingerly stepped away into the background and offered encouraging gestures and took sneaky swigs of unguarded drinks on the tables. Luci lured a couple of guards into the pub and using Baracus-Jitsu threw one of the troopers over the bar, before picking the other up by his lapels and sliding him down the bar[78].

Suzie holding the patio ground on her own produced a deck of cards to the soldiers bearing down on her and after a willing volunteer troop had picked out a card, she shuffled the pack and clubbed the unsuspecting squaddie with the deck sending them to the deck, and with great credit the card he picked was the top card doing most of the damage as he sprawled backwards (the Queen of Clubs for the record). The other troops

---

[77] Like 'pull my finger' always be wary if anyone offers you this option.

[78] Bar fight rules dictate these two things must happen.

nodded appreciatively at Suzie's sleight of hand before closing in again.

Another trooper made his way to the back and grabbed Zed by the lapels (proving that lapels are a real weak spot in a fight). Before the solider could take any further action, Zed breathed on him, the 80% proof fumes sending his assailant tumbling backwards into a table in a drunken stupor.

Alex and Captain Megaphone Operator had got themselves into a standoff, making karate style hand motions (think David Bowie dancing sometime circa 1975) as they circled each other. Neither willing to make the first move and thus expose the fact they knew nothing about fighting. In the end they settled for making vaguely rude signals at each other and doing 'don't hold me back' gestures, despite no one attempting to hold them back at all (as seen on most UK high streets late on a Saturday night).

Luci burst from the pub doors with a solider under each arm in a head lock. She weighed up whether to bang the heads together or go with the bop on the head. Who was she kidding, it was the bang the heads together every time and she joyfully swung the two together with a 'clonk'.

As this rumpus continued, the locals displaying minimum interest at best, to the shenanigans, the sound of chaos was cut across with the ring of a light metal object being tapped against a glass. Everyone immediately stopped fighting and instinctively picked up the nearest glass and raised it. Zed began to drool.

"OK that's enough!" Betty said sternly, but without anger. "OK you guys in the tin foil uniforms with the blue hats, you step that way please. And if my four friends could step to the other side of the patio please?" uncomplainingly they all moved as instructed. "Thank you. You've all had your fun, but it's now time to go your separate ways."

"But we're under orders to stop them!" said one of the troopers, judging by the volume of the voice, it was Captain Megaphone Operator.

"And you have, you've held them up for at least fifteen minutes. You can report back a success." Betty reasoned. There was a low approving murmur from the troops "go your own separate ways. And drive safely please."

With that everyone trudged (or trooped in the troops case) off exchanging various "Sorry for the knee in the testicles.", "Hope the wooden spoon in the ear wasn't too painful." Etc.

On reaching the edge of the car park Alex turned to see Betty stood on the balcony smiling at them all. She looked at Alex gave them a big beaming smile and waved. Alex mirrored her smile and waved back. With that Betty winked, turned away and disappeared from view.

Chapter E – Enough space in space to swing a Saturn IV Turbo Vole

Helena and Jane had hit rock bottom. They were bored of travel, tired of each other's company and had taken to playing tiddly winks with proximity mines to pass the time and possibly, just possibly feel something, anything. Still, all told, it beat I Spy. On the plus side they had been in space long enough to brew some high-quality ale (reasons to be cheerful and all that), which they had cracked open long before it had fully fermented.

The throne room wall intercom began to ring (to the tune 'I drove all night' by Rob Orbison in tinny polyphonic sound) over on the other side of the throne room "I mean couldn't they ring me on the intercom in the arm of the throne to save me getting up? I'm really not sure why we installed that wall mounted intercom you know" Helena mused to no one in particular.

Helena eased herself out of her throne and passed Jane sitting on the floor. "Y'ello?" she said in a posh sing song voice. "Yes, yes...yes. No, no, no...No! No, I haven't incorrectly been sold life Insurance!" Helena slammed the phone down and sighed returning to slump in her seat by Jane.

The phone began to ring again "I drove all niiiiiight to get to you, is that alriiiight..." Jane couldn't help sing along. Helena sighed again, stood up again and made her way back to the phone again.

Helena picked up the phone "What?!" Helena decided to cut out any fat pleasantries in her introduction and go for the lean approach.

"You worshipfulnesshighnessmaamm'ladyduck!" Captain Megaphone Operator was taking no chances and making sure she had the correct royal address in there somewhere.

Helena moved the phone away from her ear a little as it rang with the noise "Captain, what news? And can you turn the volume down on your phone a little, I'm getting feedback. Somehow."

"We have found the party searching for the glove and engaged them." The captain said trying to give the sentence an air of finality.

"And you stopped them?" Helena asked, her interest piqued.

"Yes" Captain Megaphone Operator replied hoping there were no follow up questions to draw out the full details.

"And you have them apprehended?" Helena cut to the specific question the good captain, the OK captain, the not great, but trying her best and slowly improving captain, didn't want to hear, or reply to.

"Arse!" She cursed.

"Sorry didn't catch that?" Helena pressed.

"Arseyes, arsyes, ar yes, yes we did!" Megaphone Operator answered, again trying to keep the detail out of her answers.

"And you still have them now?" Megaphone Operator inwardly groaned, she was tiring of Helena's ability to cut to asking the exact question she didn't want to have to answer.

"Err, no. We had to let them go. They got a really fancy solicitor in who argued we were in breach of the intergalactic law of human/xenomorph/cyborg/puppet rights. It was odd that a human lawyer was so familiar with such specific intergalactic laws, but there you go. What can you do?!" Megaphone Operator answered holding the phone tight to her chest and screwing up her face preparing for the onslaught about to come her way.

Helena felt her gorget rising, though in truth it may have been the extra spicy lamb bhuna she had eaten as part of an experimental world food breakfast.

"You what?! No look, never mind, I know how difficult it can be. Its fine, it's just how this quest seems to be going." Helena surprised herself with her measured response. Jane's eyebrows raised so high they overshot her forehead and landed round the back of her head, but quickly returned frightened at the unfamiliar view. "We're not far from Earth ourselves now, we'll find them and do what needs to be done. Wait down there and we'll forward the co-ordinates of our landing spot and meet you soon. Bye.

Bye, bye. Bye" She placed the receiver gently back.

Helena turned back to where Jane sat. A proximity mine was blinking its red warning light. "Your turn." She said matter of factly to Jane.

Chapter it: Chipping away the narrative

Finally, The Narrator found himself standing outside the village in Ashton on Mersey, where he believed the heroes had been, or would end up. Truly this was the Eldorado the Intergalactic Trip Adviser had told of. Reaching this point from immigration had been an amazing tale of daring a do and peril, with a side salad of heroism garnished with excitement cheese gratings. It would make for an amazing story in itself, if only The Narrator was any good with describing events that had happened with words.

Entering the village, a silver blur passed The Narrator. He could have sworn it was some kind of human shaped creature riding an ironing board atop a shopping trolley. What its greeting of "Cowabunga!" meant, The Narrator had no idea, but he gave a shy wave out of politeness anyway.

Asking the local residents if they'd seen some strange characters around recently was broadly met with indifference, or uncertainty to what qualified as 'strange' around these parts. Finally, giving up hope The Narrator entered a chip shop, half way up the row of shops, that had caught his eye. Given it was days since he'd last eaten a proper meal of squashed mini muffins, he was feeling decidedly hungry and could have eaten a lightly seasoned park bench, which might have been better for him than what he was gearing himself up for.

The wall of smell that hit The Narrator as he entered the chip shop started doing similar things to his stomach as the smell of sweet sick and toilet fumes from the bus ride had done days earlier. Nevertheless, he pushed on through the fug of grease to the counter in search of sustenance.

At this point the creature behind the counter harshly shouted "no chips!" at The Narrator. This toothless creature was a mask of anger and hostility radiating disdain for all life in general, The Narrator had never seen anything so beautiful in all his life.

"My good lady what a pleasure it is to have your acquaintance" he said in his smoothest register, which was about as smooth as a badger's backside when sunbathing on the worlds most jagged rock pool.

"No chips!" said the women with a fraction less hostility in her voice, though this still had more than enough hostility than required to start a war between pacifist planets.

The Narrator swallowed hard and summoned all his courage, which wasn't a lot of courage, "You beautiful rose, you delicate divine flower, what time do you knock off work so that I might have the pleasure of your exquisite company for some snacks and all being well a tonguey snog?"

"No chips!" the potato-based guardian behind the counter shouted with only a fairly thick veil of anger and contempt in her voice this time.

The Narrator smiled at her, which wasn't returned. "Madam I will reappear for you at the strike of eight pm o'clock bells.", he went to kiss her hand, saw the burning hatred at existence behind her eyes, flinched and thought better of it for now.

The Narrator smiled, turned heel and left, he would have to find a puddle to wash in and make himself presentable for this delectable creature. He still had all the sachets of shampoo he stole from the hotel which he could use for breath freshener. His mission to narrate the story was on hold, damn the fate of the universe, when he had chance of love with this unique vision of wonder.

Chapter and terse

"Your Tescoeth is not verily impressive." Stated Zed peering through the large glass doors inside. Alex took a moment to think of if there was such a thing as an impressive Tesco. Even when they discounted the fancy cheese to an actually affordable price, it barely rated above a 'meh'. Although some say the discount price cheese is but a myth as no one has ever got past the people congregating around the shelve to see the fromage based goods for themselves.

All in all, you've seen one Tesco you've seen them all Alex concluded.

"That's because its closed." Was the best Alex could manage in the end with a shrug. "Though it's not much better when its open.". Alex moved away from the doors to where Luci and Suzie were playing cat's cradle on the steps up to the car park at the side.

"Err, how long to that Moonie thing? I guess I should keep on track of that" Alex enquired. Suzie pulled a small pouch from insider her robes and took out some small bones, that Alex presumed were chicken bones, though could have been space hen for all they knew. Suzie cast them on the floor. She stared at how they fell for a few minutes and reached inside her satchel for some paper that she held up to the bones for a few minutes, her face a picture of studied concentration. She then turned the paper the other way up and stared at it for a few minutes more. Finally, she turned the paper the other way around, nodded in confirmation to herself and picked up the bones. Suzie went to speak and paused. Finally, she reached back into her knapsack and produced a calendar and looked for the date she'd ringed on it. "Tomorrow night" She confirmed having consulted the calendar.

"Right well Tesco isn't open until tomorrow morning, so we'll have to come back in the morning, first thing alas. In the meantime,…"

"…O'Neil's is just around the cornery!" Zed butted in from by the door, his hearing razor sharp on all matters alcohol related.

"NOOOO!!!!" all three chimed back in response. Clearly O'Neil's reputation of the home of the non-discerning alcoholic stretched across the Universe (Jai Guru Deva).

"Nothing for it." Alex pondered aloud. "You can all come and stay at mine."

"Won't your parents mind?" Luci asked.

"Nah my friends are their friends. Plus, it will give them an excuse to embarrass me with baby photos." With that Luci and Suzie stood up and strode past Alex. "Wait how did you know I lived with my parents…?!"

****

"Don't they look funny naked?" Alex's mum asked putting the baby photo of Alex down as Suzie and Luci nodded in unison." Didn't look much better naked as a baby" Alex's mum put in as the kicker to larks abound.

Alex's parents had taken to Alex coming home with three very strangely dressed people in the same way you would deal with a microwave vegetable lasagne when you're hungry. You're not remotely sure what it is in front of you, but you go with it anyway.

Without asking if Alex's guests were hungry, Alex's mum and dad did what most parents would do and knocked up enough food to feed the extras on the film set of The Lord of The Rings (the extended one where they drafted in the extra Orcs with a penchant for Battenburg).

Anyway, the night passed off with much hilarity, chat and novelty sized cakes. Later in the evening, Lisa came back and treated all guests like old friends proving not everyone with ambition is a soulless humour free spirit vacuum[79].

At one point in the evening, without warning there was a full-frontal attack from Helena's ground based troops who had teamed up with the Noel Edmonds aliens from the Planet Whatatit having tracked Alex's parents' home address, figuring they'd have one last crack before Helena turned up.

This battle featured superfast spaceships which did loop de loops and fired lasers and everything (and not small lasers either, large

---

[79] Mostly they are though.

ones that make a kind of 'Boowoosh' noise).
What looked like a small-scale Jean Michel
Jarre gig raged for four minutes and twenty
seconds of seat of the pants action, until Alex's
mum saw them off with a rolled-up copy of
Cheshire Life[80].

It really was an awesome battle and probably
worthy of pages of description and a couple of
sonnets, if anyone who witnessed it had any
sense.

After the fight ended, everyone had a nice cup
of Horlicks to get the violence out of aching
limbs. Turning in for the night Alex suggested
Suzie and Luci (and explicitly not Zed) could
share their bed, however this fell on blind ears
and Alex found themselves sleeping top and
tail) on an airbed with Zed in the front room.

This was disconcerting as A. Zed had an actual
tail (though to be fair he kept it neatly stowed
away in a travel bag, and B. Zed's snoring was
of such a frequency and rhythm that it caused
cats and dogs to pair up and do the
Macarena[81]. If you've never seen cats and
dogs do the Macarena, its strangely hypnotic.

After a good nights sleep (except for the cats
and dogs in the area who were all knackered
after a night of dancing in unison) our
adventurers ate a breakfast that was so beige,
it was the colour of an unambitious elderly

---

[80] A magazine that if it were any more vacuous would pull the
world into itself like some sort of black hole.
[81] Other dated 90's dance craze references are available.

ladies' bathroom in the 1970s. With that, Alex's mum wished them luck with the whole save the planet thing and sent them off with an oversized pack lunch and a sloppy kiss on the cheek.

Another Chapter bites the dust – Blue Caps means full fat

Admiral Theview stood on the hull, why that North Eastern part of England had been put into his ship, he had never asked. His uniform was crisply ironed with a secondary peanutly bit of ironing to cover all the snack bases. He had his 128 medals pinned to his chest which meant the weight caused him to constantly stoop forward. He was looking forward to the day someone invented back medals to balance things out. He had awarded most of the medals to himself, but he had definitely earned the 'hero of the toast' award, as he did make amazingly average buttered toast.

He was very proud of his career and that he had made it to the rank of rear middle second from the back twice removed Admiral, shortened to Admiral to save everyone time, unless the full Admiral was around at which point things got a little more complicated. It had taken him years to get the necessary (and heavily liberal with the truth) examples of how he was best placed to be in charge of the fleet for the job application.

Though when he allowed himself to admit it, it was worrying him a little that he was in charge of an entire fleet of ships without understanding how one actually worked, let alone an entire fleet. And space. Space scared him. A lot. It was pretty big and had lots of physics rules you had to follow otherwise you would die in a variety of unpleasant ways. Still the space fleet board had decreed his heavily liberal with the truth (as we've already established) examples of how he was uniquely qualified to lead a fleet, as exactly the kind of credentials someone in charge of a fleet might have.

Admiral Theview's second in command approached "Dick Head[82] we have orders from Queen Helena."

Theview turned to face Semi-Commander Smith-Sunshine "What orders?"

"Well Dick Head she wants us to head to Earth and take out the collective seeking to deprive her of the glove of ultimate power. The previous troops have failed and Helena is hoping we can success where they have failed so she can turn around and go home" The Semi-Commander confirmed committedly.

"Hmmm" Theview contemplated, pretending he understood every, or indeed any, of the words just said to him. He didn't have the faintest clue where, or what Earth was, or how to find it, which was a bit like not knowing where it was. He would go ask Sub Trainee navigator Froude, the lowest ranked person on board who was in charge of making sure the ship got safely to where it was meant to.

Approaching the comms desk at the front of the cockpit he neared a dishevelled colleague who couldn't have looked less military precise if his

---

[82] Blue Caps terms for addressing superior were 'quirky' at best.

gun had been bent to face back at him. "Now Froude,I have a specific order for you. I need to get to Earth. Immediately. Make it so" The Admiral commanded confidently.

"Well Dick Head, which Earth do you want to get to? The real Earth or the fake Earth of the 'Earth World' theme park on Planet Westworld Four? Or do you mean earth in the ground? And when you say immediately do you mean in this time frame, or that of if you travelled through a black hole? You've got to pick your paradigms."

The Admiral was flummoxed by all these words "Well I…"

"….We could try and find a warp gate and look for an alternative Earth, but that would still very much fit the broad description of Earth and if we were lucky we might travel back in time and get there before we were needed, thus fitting the 'immediately' part of our remit and better. Although, strangely, if we could go via Maroon 5^{83}, as there is a dust cloud, we can sling shot off that and we'll get there four hours quicker again, so as management, what are you choosing. You tell me the co-ordinates and I'll punch them in."

Theview felt his face flushing "Which co-ordinates…err…what…now look just get me to planet Earth quickly!" he stammered.

---

[83] A barren soulless planet.

"You're asking the wrong question." Froude rebutted him.

"And what is the right question?" Theview asked back, just about suppressing his ire at this tedious dance.

"Well it depends. You get what you ask for. You need to consider if you really want to go to Earth. You managers make all these decisions without knowing what you properly want. Have you considered the state of the Vespina belt? So, what I'm saying to you is…"

At this point Theview had given it up as a bad lot, walking away from Froude mid-sentence (not that Froude appeared to notice) and strolling over to Captain Saxon-Prince "Captain, I have a development opportunity for you."

"Dick Head!" Saxon-Prince snapped his heels together followed by his elbows then his eyebrows for full Mexican Wave effect.

"Captain, I see so much potential in you. You are easily more than capable of reaching Admiral grade." Theview lied, Saxon-Prince had as much Admiral potential as a wonkily built helter-skelter on the side of a crumbling mountain made of Digestive biscuit. "We need to get to Earth, make it so.".

Saxon-Price saluted and made his way through the hub to Froude. Theview stayed back and watched intently as they engaged in a conversation for ten minutes, maybe fifteen, more like twelve, if you were to put a stopwatch to it. Ultimately an ashen faced Saxon-Prince turned away and strode purposefully to Miami Vice Admiral Ram-man who was stood watching the radar pretending he understood its readings.

After they had exchanged words, Ram-man walked over to Froude. An exchange began, Ram-man cocked is head to one side and stroked his chin as Froude spoke at him. After twenty minutes of this, Ram-man returned to Saxon-Prince. Presently Saxon-Prince and Ram-man approached the Admiral "it is done." Spoke Saxon-Prince with a nervous tone in his voice.

At this point several colours of brown filled the command centre, followed by the sound of offbeat xylophone music accompanied by turkeys squawking hip hop beats, the ship sped up immeasurably[84].

"I hate hyperspace." Theview mused as the ship came to a shuddering halt. The three officers stared out of the viewing portal, outside the spaceship was a large ball of flame and two elks playing indifferent rocket pants table tennis.

"Where are we?!" Barked Theview.

"We're...we're not sure." Chief Navigation officer Sgt-Hawkins responded looking at a

---

[84] It probably did get measured on the speedometer on the dashboard of the ship truth be told.

variety of red blinking lights on the desk in front of him.

Theview leaned on the rail of the command area "Exactly as I planned it" he declared "We wait here, and our quarry comes to us. Entirely as I intended".

Chapter under – Every little (from a farmer bullying multi billion pound company) helps

"I won't do it. I *can't* do it" Alex repeated the words like a mantra as they paced awkwardly outside the main doors to the Sale branch of Tesco.

"It's OK." Suzie said super soothingly (she may also sell seashells by the sea shore and all that). "Having the fate of the entire world on your shoulders is a burden many would struggle to comprehend, much less take on." She grabbed Alex affectionately on the shoulder "but don't panic, you can do this. And you've got all of us to help you" She glanced worryingly at Zed "Luci and I totally have your back".

"No, no." Alex responded "I mean I won't be one of those people stood outside a supermarket waiting for it to open first thing in the morning. This isn't Dawn of the Dead. I collect beer bottle tops as a hobby, but even I've not sunk so low as to spend my time pressed against a door waiting for a supermarket to open, its madness." Alex exhaled and shook their head.

The four turned their gaze to the imposing glass doors closed in front of them.

"No offence" Alex said to some bored looking locals milling around the doors. Their apology was met with some kind of groaned indifferent shrug.

Luci regarded Alex with one eye. As she was a highly trained lethal assassin, this caused minor bowel movement in Alex. "This is the first time you've shown passion. For anything!" she said with a possible hint of pride in her voice.

"I have standards. They're incredibly low, but I have standards." Alex sniffed.

Suzie rubbed her chin. "OK how about we pretend we're town planners until the store opens? Would that help?"

Alex considered this for a moment. Picked their nose, then declared "Works for me." With that, the four took up strategic positions on the precinct looking down the line of their thumbs and making viewing screens with their hands (mistaking town planning for directing films, or just being a pretentious prat).

This gambit was broken by the swish of automatic doors opening behind them. The heroes turned just in time as the last of the locals entered within muttering something about it being a disgrace that the store had opened two minutes late at 6:02. The group followed on entering the store looking keenly, with Zed immediately turning his attention to finding the alcohol section, not realising it was always the furthest aisle in an (failed) attempt to deter British alcoholism metre by metre.

"So, what is a sub cheese counter?" Suzie mused as they stood in front of the newspaper stand just inside the store.

"No idea." Alex started. And ended. Bringing nothing to the conversation.

"Well sires, if you will alloweth me." Zed also began, but unlike Alex had the courage of his convictions to see this one through "There is a legend of the great intergalactic war of the fax machines. A battle to reamaineth relevant despite their obsolescence in anything other than football transfers. One side verily did build a submarine made of the pongiest stilton. This battle vessel was called 'Live and rennet live', a submarine of purest cheese..." Zed paused, took in the faces of his companions and even he realising in his potion addled mind that he'd lost them. "No, I've no ideaeth either." Zed conceded defeat though there was not too much shame in that as the others had pretty much ceased to pay his story attention from to him from commencement of the word 'well'.

"Seems simple to me" Luci mused, "We find the cheese counter and go from there". And you know what? That's what they did, they found the cheese counter and went from there. And coming up is what happened when they hit 'from there'.

As they walked down the aisle containing so many types of yoghurts (that all essentially taste the same in the end), Alex stopped; "You know I'm not really comfortable with this whole saviour of the world thing. Seems like it might carry a little responsibility and expectation.

"You're right." concurred Luci "This Tesco is horrid." And with that she carried on walking. Suzie followed closely behind and gave Alex a smile on her way past. Alex shrugged seemingly beaten.

After minutes interrogating and searching the cheese counter (and by that, I mean trying as many free samples as they felt they could get away with), the four were beginning to lose hope.

"Hey you!" Shouted a reedy nasal voice. The four looked at each other to see where this source had come from. "Are you looking for a clue to something significant?" The disembodied voice came back again.

"Oh yes mightyeth voice thing!" Zed bellowed to the skies.

"Down here beardy!" the voice responded. The group bent down and underneath the cheese counter was a small, tiny in fact, cheese counter selling a variety of cheeses in miniature form. There was a baby bel at the back of the counter that looked like a tractor tyre (the really big ones that get all the cow poo stuck in the grooves) by comparison. Behind the counter in an apron and hair net stood a goblin, well it's difficult to say what he was but you know, small, green, pointy ears, long nose, beady eyes, consulting a Warhammer bestiary, Dungeons and Dragons rule book and most Tolkien literature, this creature was pinned as a

Goblin. Or maybe a Boglin (or any other anagram of those letters, a Noblig maybe?).

"Surprise!" the goblin shouted cheerfully stretching out its arms in an ostentatious pose. The heroes looked at each other and gave a combined shrug. Suzie's was a particular elaborate shrug involving full arm rotation head tilt and puffing out of the cheeks. "Bet you weren't expecting me eh? Pretty freaky no?"

"Meh!" Alex replied dismissively "I've been hanging around with aliens these last couple of days, so it takes something pretty considerable truth be told. Wait you guys are aliens, right?"

"Depends on your perspective." Suzie replied not wanting to get drawn into that discussion right now.

"Ether way" Alex picked up the thread again "I've had a fairly bonkers last couple of days. They've put the price of the cider up by 20p in the Weatherspoon's for a start, never saw that one coming. I'm pretty unshockable these days"

"What?!" The goblin seemed genuinely taken back and shocked "this won't do, I'm always a big surprise, people look on me with awe, and a little disgust, no this will not do". The goblin folded its arms across its chest in thought.

"What would you have us do my goblin liege?" Zed asked the creature.

"Start again!" the goblin decided uncrossing his arms and clapping his hands together.

"What?!" Luci asked ~~exaaacerbated~~, ~~excsasabated~~, ~~excassabated~~, flustered. "We're going to do no such thing you little green turd!"

"Do you want this clue or not?" The goblin teased knowing its position of strength, "Go out of the store, find me again and appear shocked when you do. I want genuine surprise, I've starred in an Am Dram version of Mother Goose so I know authenticity in an act when I see it."

The group exchanged looks. Suzie took out a compact mirror to confirm that she was indeed trapped in this tedious situation, her reflection confirmed so. The heroes turned on their heels and made their way to the door, smiling at the security guard on stood there to cause maximum paranoia in him. Reaching the newspaper stand just where they had originally milled around when arriving, they turned to go back to the cheese counter. Mid first step the tannoy started up with a short burst of (cliched) feedback.

"Alan here. Did we establish my name was Alan in our exchange? You may have gleaned that some other information perhaps? Well either way, my name is Alan the goblin and manager of the sub cheese counter. Do it properly, I can see from CCTV you're still in the store, go out and come back in again."

"I'd sigh but fear I'd never stop" Luci declared flatly, or apartmently if you're an estate agent. "Lets just get this over and done with, that

193

moon comes up tonight." The four obeyed the snot green monster leaving the store, coming straight back in and presently finding themselves crouching back at the small counter.

"Surprise!" shouted the goblin as they approached.

"Oh would you look at that." Suzie replied, her voice as flat as a sumo wrestler driving an especially big steamroller in Holland.

"So, you'll want a clue, yes?" the goblin probed.

"May as well while we're here." Alex responded their heart (and most major organs) not really in this exchange.

"Right." The goblin reached into his surprisingly smart pair of chinos, producing a crumpled piece of paper he unfolded it gingerly and read; "Super noodles, Lloyd Grossman pasta sauce, cat litter, bling blong platinum hair dye for Mrs goblin…oh wait sorry that's my shopping list, I best not forget any of that or I'll be in trouble with the missus." He scrunched the paper back up and placed it in his back pocket. Looking mildly flustered, he scanned around the counter.

"Mr Goblin Esquire" Zed began, "I believe you doth hath framedest it behind you".

The goblin spun and there on the wall next to his goblin employee of the month award (for passable hygiene standards and near acceptable customer service) was a frame with 'the clue' written on it in Crayola. The rest of the document was written in tiny font, more irritating still it was default Calibri. The goblin plucked the frame off the wall and returned to the counter where he threw the frame hard to the floor. The frame landed with a loud flat splat. The goblin looked non plussed muttering something about "plastic front, thought it was glass. Well that's the dramatic smashed opening buggered." He proceeded to huffily pull the back of the frame off getting sore nails from pulling the metal holders back.

Luci sidled over to Luci, "When do we get to have our own adventure away from all this?" she asked. Suzie pulled a face that said 'the day can't come soon enough, I'm a powerful magician reduced to dealing with small green things at a tiny cheese counter in a dull suburb of South Manchester', it truly was a face pull for the ages.

The goblin coughed to ensure he had everyone's attention, gauging the faces he wasn't sure he did, but went with it anyway. "OK here goes, you know Harborough park?" Alex nodded "well press down the allotted dog turd and the resting place of the glove will be revealed."

"Woah, woah roll back a minute!" Suzie started, attention not so much grabbed as border line sexual harassed "the button is shaped like, like a dog poo?"

"The scripture says nothing of the button being dog poo *shaped*." The goblin corrected Suzie.

"So, we have to press an as yest unidentified dog turd to reveal the glove?" Luci asked wide eyed and more than a little disgusted.

"It's Harborough park, its full of dog turds!" Alex howled "I mean really is this the best they could come up with? Was there nothing on which one and where it actually is?"

"No!" said the goblin in a voice that brooked no argument.

Luci ignored the brook via a conveniently located bridge and asked, "So we're expected to go around pressing dog mess?"

The goblin considered the question. "pretty good security if you ask me, how many people actively look to engage with dog turds?" He turned to the counter at the side "Now if you could leave me, I have some stilton to bag up for the discount section. Good days sirs." Alex went to ask another question "I said good day sirs!" barked the goblin.

The four turned and began to trudge off "Hiding a button under a dog poo, what kind of weak mind comes up with such childish claptrap?" Luci asked staring into the middle distance.

Zed stroked his beard and mused "I thought it quite clever thyself."

With that, the four left the store, but not before going past the discount section (fighting their way through the throng of people gawping at the yellow stickers offering them pence off an item they don't like that they weren't intending to buy) and picking up some two days past best egg and cress sandwich for 37p less.

This adventure was going to end as it started. Total shit.

Chapter ahoy: Like a bad game of Trivial Pursuit there are more questions than answers aka Doomed to Fail Cheese Hunt

The four sorta heroes trudged down Barker's Lane looking to cut through to Harboro park. All four were in silence, their minds set on the task that lay ahead and the fate of the universe. Actually Zed's was probably set on when he could have his next drink, but he was definitely focused on something.

Reaching the point on the road where a large painted black and white gothic type house was on their left Alex pulled up "You know, I've been thinking".

Luci looked them over "it doesn't suit you mate" she said finally with a smirk.

Alex ignored the slight and continued "So this glove which has so much potential danger for everyone was entrusted with The Quizzicals and as far as I can tell, they've hidden all the clues *and* the glove itself in the same town, within a couple of miles of each other? Surely the whole of the universe was available to them and they could have split the clues and glove much further afield which may have slowed people down or put them off? I mean its just lazy location work?"

Suzie put her hands on her hips and considered the question "You know, we just have to trust The Quizzicals on this one, they know the danger represented and they would have put their best people on it."

Alex shrugged and started walking again, "here is the other thing, you're all from another planet right? And yet you all look essentially like normal humans…" Alex glanced to the side at Zed "…mostly, and you speak English like me. I always thought given the infinite nature of the universe, you know, you might look and sound a little different? There might be a bit more variety at play?"

Luci laughed "And how do you know we're not wearing some kind of hi-tech alien skin cloaking device?" she turned and gave Alex a deliberate odd stare that unnerved them a little and then in the spookiest voice she could manage "Wooooo!", all four broke out into a laugh.

Alex kicked their feet through the leaves in front of them "so how did you get here?" they asked.

"Well my liege verily in the beginning there waseth a giant life giving baked potato…"Zed began.

"…No, no" Alex cut across, worried where this story of creation was going "How did you get to Earth, must have been some journey, no planets in this solar system with life on them according to our scientists so that's some distance to come. Your first time on this planet?"

"In my case, it was public transport" Luci began "Intergalactic train and coach, but seriously, who wants a story about a Megabus journey?" she did a little spin as she walked "First time on this pokey little planet? I could tell you, but then I'd have to atomise your soul from existence!" Again Luci laughed as did Alex still not entirely sure of if Luci was kidding, she was not easy to read where jokes and painful death were concerned.

"You saw my vessel" Suzie stated, "I had a lovely little pootle here in that thing, listening to my favourite Space Power Ballads 'Total Eclipse of The Planet Phart', 'Eternal Flame Rocket', 'French Kissing in G'wanmyson Five'. And my people get around, so I reckon they've been to Earth before, but for me, first time. I'm very impressed with your street lights, I'll be telling everyone back home about those".

"Zed?" Alex asked, Zed snapped out of what appeared to be a trance state, though it could just have equally been he was being gormless.

"Ah my liege, you also saw how I gots hereth" Zed said, brushing over the fact no one had been entirely satisfied with his story of him getting towed here "As for the first timely, nay not at all-est. First time I came thy saw lots of biggy lizardseth roaming around, that doth truly a fun time!" Zed said and didn't expand any further on his answer and none of the gang were sure they wanted to probe further.

After a pause Alex spoke again "Either way, thanks all for coming and helping out, I'm sure you're doing your home planets proud. Its good that in times of need no matter where you're from you've come together to help, to do right"

And with that no more was said as the gang made their way onto Harboro road with a renewed sense of purpose.

Chapter dis – The Woman who carefully landed on Earth

"Careful now, careful now. CAREFUL NOW!" Helena instructed/bellowed at the pilot backing the twenty five story, twin turreted, conservatory extensioned spaceship into the parking bay at the street. "Make sure you're within three inches of the kerb."

"Bloody back throne drivers." Muttered the pilot.

Against all laws of physics, gravity and a couple of chemistry, the ship fit perfectly in the one car gap.

"Does anyone understand parking restrictions?" Helena asked seeing a sea of blank faces in the command centre, "Are we OK as its after 5pm on a weekday?". After much discussion amongst the crew it was decided they would be OK as A. The spaceship had no registration plate, B. It had no windscreen to stick the ticket on and C. The defence laser system would obliterate any unauthorised person touching the ship. And they'd set the laser to 'anti traffic warden' mode to make extra sure.

Taking the exit ramp (they had toyed with the exit fireman's pole or exit dodgem car, but decided to stay traditional for this mission) Helena, Jane and some elite troops exited outside onto a non descript suburban road. Helena stared up at the 90-metre-tall high gothic (with a hit of Art Deco to keep it fresh) architecture of her command ship "remember where we parked." Helena asked and Jane nodded dutifully.

Captain Megaphone and her elite troops, who had been killing time playing boule at Wythenshawe Park, zeroed in on the ships co-ordinates to join this war party.

"So how do you think we find them my Queen?" Jane asked.

"Errrr…" Helena pondered unphilosophically.

"Well I was going to save this for one of your birthdays[85], but…" Jane started coyly but finished carply "…the scientist you disliked and banished to the planet Two For One Sausage Rolls[86]" Helena eyed Jane suspiciously "Well he left this 'Hero-find-a-tron 2000', which, I assume, does what it says on the packaging." Helena took the box from Jane.

"It's plastic shrink wrapped, let me just peel here, no maybe here…wait what if I get my nail under here" Helena and Jane picked wildly at the box (the only thing in the galaxy more impenetrable than plastic wrap is the Big Up Yourself forcefield on Planet Chastity Belt). Ultimately, Helena declared for a guard to go in and get a kitchen lightsabre.

1 hours 55 minutes later…

---

[85] As previously established, rulers on the planet Eccles have a lot of birthdays.
[86] Not the worst planet to be stranded on, that would be the planet Bud Lite.

"We're in!" Helena declared triumphantly, as seven of her guard lay dead around her "Oh wait we need to charge it!"

5 hours later…

"OK so we have 1 bar of power, your highness hopefully that's enough." Jane stated handing the device to Helena. Helena switched on the device and pressed the options button.

10 hours later…

"OK your highness, so we have 3 bars of power, that's got to be enough".

Helena thumbed the device and pressed the options button again. "Alright, I'm guessing I press the 'make this thing work' button?" she asked rhetorically with an edge of doubt in her voice. As a Queen, working devices wasn't really her speciality. With that, the device whirred into life with a few impressive looking buttons blinking on and off like a futuristic fruit machine. Eventually a gravely Scottish voice (that big ginger bloke who is in everything to do with Scotland, presumably as the machine's budget couldn't stretch to Sean Connery or at a pinch, Billy Connolly) barked out in polyphonic speakers "they're heading to Harborough park. G'night." And promptly switched itself off to save using up the last bar of battery life.

"We must head to this park of wonder. Now!" Helena bellowed. "Driver set coordinates" She yelled up the ramp into the ship.

The driver who had been admiring his parking, put down his brew, re rolled up his copy of The Daily Dwarf Star and put the choke in to start the engine. He added the strangle as well to give full power. "I'm more of a pilot really." He muttered.

Chapter here - Confidence is a preference for the habitual voyeur, Of what is known as (parklife!), And morning soup can be avoided, If you take a route straight through what is known as (parklife!), John's got brewers droop he gets intimidated by the dirty pigeons, They love a bit of it (parklife), Who's that gut lord marching? You should cut down on your pork life mate, Get some exercise! All the people, so many people, and they all go hand in hand. Hand in hand through their (crappy) park life. Park life, park life, park life, PARK LIFE!

"OK, we're here". Said Alex opening the gate in the corner of the park.

Chapter 144142451158788841154441444 - (Emily) Attak of the (Martin) Clunes.

"Take that and *that*!" high intensity sparks flew leaving only smoke and cordite in the air stinging the nostrils[87]. "Try to hide, would you?" another spark "Ah and the last one! I've been waiting for you my so called chosen one friend and now your adventure is over!". A final blinding spark filled the cockpit with a glowing intensity before fading out, leaving the room in near pitch black. "And that. That is how you vanquish your enemies." Helena exclaimed unable to hide her triumph (And not small amount of smugness) in her voice. She surveyed the destruction she had wrought in front of her. Turning from her game of whack a mole she faced Jane and smiled; "What do you think?".

"Highly impressive your...err highness,". A pause hung in the air, though if you looked closely enough you could see the fine thread suspending it. "do you think we should try and get the glove of power now?" Jane asked politely.

"What? Hmmm yes, we've come this far I suppose we should finish the job. Driver, pilot, chauffeur, astronaut, whatever, set the co-ordinates!".

The pilot having already got them to their destination, but not wanting to contradict the

---

[87] Think Brut, but less unpleasant smelling.

queen, pressed some none important buttons[88] (windscreen wipers, toilet flush, Hyperion credit reference check, interplanetary death ray etc.) and made some engine noises with his mouth. "We're here." After a few minutes of the charade, he declared. And indeed, they were. Always.

---

[88] The type a DJ lets his mate next to him on the decks press to feel involved.

You can't always get what you want, not without pressing a few dog poos first.

Dusk was setting, the dull sun retreating to happier times over the horizon. Alex looked down at the brown shape below their feet, trying to hold their breath and repeating some kind of mantra about the fate of the universe being in (their about to be heavily soiled) hands. "Is this really the best they could come up with?" Alex asked someone, anyone, the void probably. The other three paid no heed and continued to scour the field (scour may be stretching it, given how covered in dog muck it was) for the button that would reveal all.

Alex held their breath, held their nose, held their nerve, held their own, bent over and pressed their finger I to the dog poo trying to ignore the disconcerting feeling of warmth passing up their digit. This was it, the grand plan would surely be revealed.

Nothing. Alex stuffed their hand in their pockets in frustration and then remembered their finger "Oh for f…!"

"Anything?" Suzie asked breezily, bordering on cheerily.

"No and I've no desire to keep sticking my fingers in dog poo in the hope of finding a button that will reveal a glove of supposed power to rule the universe!" Alex declared angrily.

"If I had a pound for every time I heard that sentence…" Luci muttered over by the hedge next to the road.

"Fingers Alex?" Suzie asked confused. She showed Alex the stick she had been using to press into the dog muck to Alex. In the background Zed waved an elaborate branch (that appeared to still be attached to the tree) he was using to Alex.

"That's not going to work." Alex stated, "the legend said very clearly we had to use our fingers to press the button hidden in a dog poo."

"Where did it say that Alex?" Suzie asked genuinely confused, Alex saw Luci making no attempt to stifle her laugh, as her shoulders rocked, and she spun the stick in her fingers around her head in the background.

"It said very clearly on the…the part where…it was written… you all saw the bit. Oh for f…"

"There is a stick overeth there squire! Zed pointed happily (if a point can be happy) at a twig under a tree.

Alex sighed "I've come this far; I'm sticking to my technique." Adventures were overrated and Alex had decided whoever set this one in motion was a complete burk.

As dusk settled in, Alex walked to the far end of the park from the gate they'd entered to clear their head and lungs. An especially large piece of dog mess caught their eye and they strolled over to it.

Alex took a deep breath inhaling deeply, before coughing repeatedly as the fumes filled their nostrils. Alex expelled their breath as quickly as possible, took a couple of steps to the side and inhaled shallowly instantly feeling that was the better decision. Having got their breath back, Alex stepped back bent down and pressed in.

Again nothing.

Alex sighed, spun and started to stroll towards the other three who were taking an unofficial breather by the swings, drinking from a thermos Zed had pulled from, well Alex didn't want to think where that thermos had come from.

Moving away, Alex heard a click, then a clack, possibly a cluck and then finally a low rumbling as the ground began to gently thrum. Alex instantly spun 360 degrees realising this brought them facing back the same way they started. Alex tried a 180-degree spin.

Luci, Suzie and Zed tepid footed over to Alex and all four stood staring in awe as where the dog poo had been, a column was beginning to rise and rise from the ground. It must have been fifty feet in diameter and as it continued to reach for the sky it must have been two hundred metres high (unlike its diameter, its height falling in step with the metric system) when it finally rested from its movement.

"I hope they've got planning permission for that!" said a grumpy resident staring over the hedge.

The moon decided at this point to make a guest appearance from behind a cloud, its beam hitting the lower part of the column.

"My liege, that's it!" Zed stated excitedy, proving his bachelor honours degree in the bleedin' obvious hadn't been wasted.

Chapter 20 – If you read only one chapter in this book, it should probably be this one.

All four heroes stood staring up, mouths agape, at the column stretching high above them.

"We have to climb *that*?" Alex asked incredulous.

"We?!" Luci echoed "You're the chosen one. Crack on!" she gave Alex a gentle shove (which given Luci's strength nearly dislocated Alex's shoulder and their big toe) towards the column.

Alex stared around. Seeing none of their companions making any kind of movement they sighed and muttered "shitbags" under their breath. Luci changed tack and patted Alex on the back partly in encouragement and partly to wipe a bit of dog muck off her hand. Suzie offered a warm smile and a Murray mint to Alex. Zed was just staring into space, possibly as far as Neptune, as his alcohol levels started to drop to seriously low levels (about only 60% of his bloodstream).

Alex drew themselves to their full self-portrait height and strode purposefully to the column whistling The Highlander theme music as they went. The column cast an imposing moonlit shadow, Alex reached its base and placed a hand on it. The column was cold and hard to the touch, much like an over-frozen breaded cod. Feeling around, Alex found a hand grip just above their head and with great exertion hauled themselves up, another tiny handgrip revealed itself to the left and Alex grasped this and pulled themselves up a little further again, however, their grip started to slip, Alex flailed, but to no avail and they were sent plummeting to the park below.

Alex hit the ground from the three-foot drop with a thud much heavier than the height dictated.

"Alex!" Suzie yelled, even though she didn't need to as she was only stood four foot away. "Use the stairs you pillock!" she said showing no concern for the drop Alex had just taken, which was probably fair enough given how low down the fall had been from.

Alex took a full sweep of the column, indeed starting from the left (Right if you were stood on the other side of the column) was a staircase circling the entire column, ascending. The staircase had an impressively ornate bannister and a slightly tatty patterned carpet.

Alex shuffled over to the staircase and started to climb, climb, climb. Each exertion of the steps causing the lactic acid to bite deep in their thighs. Risking a look down, Alex found themselves face to face with Zed who had his head pressed against the bannister.

"Keep going thy boss, thy master, thy mistress, thy champion!" he encouraged nonsensically.

Alex inwardly let out a groan, though some may have escaped from their ear, at the four foot of progress made so far. Alex steeled themselves, the fate of the entire Universe and Sale rested on their slender shoulders. Failure was not an option. Yet.

Gripping the bannister, knuckles whitening, Alex pressed on, determination passing through each step. After another eight steps, Alex took a seat for a breather.

"What time is dawn?" Luci asked through gritted teeth to Suzie.

"Swings?" Suzie countered back. Luci smiled and nodded and with that, the world's most dangerous assassin and powerful wizard held hands and skipped to the other end of the park where the swings were located. Sitting themselves in they started to push off higher, and higher, feeling the exhilaration of weightlessness.

"Oi you two, stop having fun!" a local resident yelled from a window over the road at the two of them.

"Best show willing eh?" Suzie turned to the swing to her left and asked Luci, Luci nodded and the two congad[89] back to the column to see Alex rising ever higher, now at least twelve foot off the ground. Zed had kept himself occupied making a daisy chain. Nettles lay strewn around him, demonstrative of an aborted attempt to make nettle wine.

---

[89] A two-person conga truly a tragic sight. Like being the only person in the room doing the Time warp.

"How are you doing?" Suzie asked. Alex responded in a series of panting sounds.

"Cool Darth Vader impression!" Suzie yelled back encouragingly. Alex gave Suzie daggers, a few knives, a stiletto and a letter opener to be on the safe side.

Ever onwards Alex pushed, each step more painful than the last, but determination kicked in knowing that a few people were counting on them.

"How far have I got?" Alex bellowed down optimistically.

"About nine metres up!" Luci responded in her most encouraging voice.

"Right. Time to throw up!" Alex bellowed back quoting the ancient Chinese philosopher Dr Venkman. Alex went to take another seat, but by sheer chance, a lost giant space bat flew under the column creating a strong gust underneath Alex catching their jacket like a parachute, sending them up the stairs in double quick time. Confused at this turn of events, the space bat used its wings to create a kind of shrug and sped off to Rhyll, where it had a date with an especially well travelled Albatross.

Hope crept through Alex's body as the bannister seemed to end. Yes, they had reached the top. The platform was a smooth marble that stretched out. In a nice touch there was a welcome mat at the top of the stairs with 'no place like home' written across it. The platform was empty save for a strange console at the far end, that Alex couldn't make out the full details of in the light.

Staring up, Alex saw the moon high above emerge from a cloud, its light casting on the edge of the platform.

Alex steeled themselves, realised they'd done this before so went for aluminiuming themselves as it was cheaper and easier to recycle. Probably. Alex took two purposeful steps towards the column. Stopped, turned around going back to wipe their feet on the mat, and strolled back to the column, mixing purposeful steps with some ambivalent steps.

The column in the corner was perfectly cylindrical, smooth around the sides and rose three foot to the top where an indentation was in the panel. "I got this, Total Recall, the good Paul Veerhoven one, just stick your hand in and it works it magic. Easy!" Alex said triumphantly as they stepped close the console. Looking down, the alien hand indentation was replaced with what looked suspiciously like a bottom indentation. "Oh this is just moronic!" Alex howled at the moon. The moon declined to comment.

"What did they say?" Luci asked below.

"I think Alex said 'I'm on it'" Suzie guessed.

"I thought they said, 'thou is me eth'" Zed stated a number of nettles dangling from his mouth. Suzie and Luci ignored him and the statement that made not one jot of sense.

Back up top, Alex stared at the podium, grimaced, grit their teeth, pulled a few faces, realised gurning wasn't the way forward, dropped their pants around their ankles and backed up to the indentation. Clearly the Quizzicals had read too much into the significance of the 'moon's' involvement in this process.

"Not so fast!" a cold voice cut across the night as Helena appeared out of a clearly signposted and prominent lift that traversed up and down the column (that Alex had somehow completely missed) with a cold look in her eyes.

The Chapter with no name. Other than this

Jesse Samson eased his way up the dull brown carpeted stairs, nursing a cup of tea in one hand and a plate of chocolate Hob Nobs in the other. Whistling a surprisingly effective multi harmonised version of 'Our Friends Electric', as he went along. He walked straight down the landing to the door at the end. Entering, he placed his tea and plate just so on the desk in front of him. He turned his computer on enjoying the familiar low hum as it came to life.

He reached into the top draw of this desk retrieving his notebook. Today was the day he was going to write the greatest story ever told, a fable that would alter the lives of all that read it forever. He carefully dunked a Hob Nob in the brew, trusting the integrity of the biscuit against the degenerative powers of the hot liquid.

He pondered how best to tell his tale in a way that mortals could comprehend and grasp the complexities of the truths (and a few good fart jokes thrown in for good measure) it would reveal, when his thought process was broken by a loud smashing noise as Helena burst through the window at the right of his office.

"No! No!! No!!! No more distractions from finishing the story!" She bellowed face red and contorted with rage. She snatched Jesse's notebook up from their hand and dropped it on the floor and stamped on it a couple of times. With that she ran out of the door screaming "Aaarrrggghhhh!!" as she went, her voice eventually fading down the landing and then the stairs. Jesse listened to her voice going until silence met him. He picked up the notebook that was not damaged in any material way by this strange attack. He then turned his attention to his Hob Nob just as it broke in two and fell in his brew.

"Bollocks."

This Chapter - Love you to the Moon and back, but I'll need to stop at a service station at some point on the journey as I need a toilet break and a Twix

At the bottom of the pillar the three grounded (well reasonably grounded, they had their odd moments of flights of fancy) heroes formed a battle stance line against Helena's troops who had descended on them and were encircling. Luci was windmilling her arms, Suzie looking in her top hat for the right angry animal to conjure and Zed just looking a little confused but smiling out of politeness to the new arrivals.

Jane stepped forward, a legion of Helena's mightiest battalion right behind her. She halted and raised her arm, the troops held up behind her. A pause swept across the battlefield (well park) as the two sides weighed each other seeing who was going to make the first move. Muscles flexed on weapons and sinews grew taught. The sense of anticipation on both sides was almost suffocating.

Finally the spell was broken as Jane gave it her best attempt (bless her) at a military command "TAKE THEM!" she screamed at the top of her voice (which carried surprisingly well given her diminutive stature), before adding "please" as the soldiers poured past her heading towards Luci, Suzie and Zed with weapons raised.

****

Helena pulled a blastatron blasty blaster from her pocket which caught Alex by surprise as her snug looking space pants didn't seem so roomy. Helena took aim. Paused. Then decided to go with the 'cool' shooting the gun sideways approach, firing off a round as she twisted her gun to the side. Alex yelped and leapt off the console as a laser bolt whistled in the wrong key past where their head had just been.

Alex rolled and gained their feet in a surprisingly not entirely awful movement. Turning they saw Helena training her gun on them. Alex looked around the platform, there was no cover anywhere. There wasn't even a valance. Alex put up their hands and backed away across the smooth floor. Helena kept her gaze on Alex, her fingers playing close to the trigger. Alex continued to back up until they felt their heels touching the edge of the platform. Alex turned and saw their plight below if they took another step backwards.

"You did well Terran, better than I expected of your pitiful race." Helena began "to solve all those fiendish clues and end up here, so close to having all that power."

"Moronic!" Alex responded as a kind of challenge.

"Huh?" Helena asked surprised.

"The clues were moronic" Alex clarified defiantly.

"Never mind, that's not important now. To come this close shows why you were rightly the chosen one. But ultimately all you've done is the leg work for me. Soon I will have the glove and rule all the galaxy and…"

"…Here we go." Alex interrupted rolling their eyes.

"What?! I mean, I beg your pardon?" Helena blustered taken aback. To about 1997 at a guess.

"You've descended into cliché. I've seen this film so many times. The villain revealing all their plans at the point they think they've won. Spare me, I've dealt with enough space arse these last couple of days." Alex held Helena's stare.

"So be it…" Helena's gaze hardened and she started to squeeze the trigger "…chosen one."

Alex held their head high "Do you know why I'm the chosen one?" Helena paused in pulling the trigger and looked perplexed, Alex continued "It's as I always give up." And with that Alex took a step back and disappeared over the edge of the column.

Chapter hear me now! - Total Power corrupts and a little power corrupts a lot more than it should – ask any middle manager

Unaware of the fate of the world playing above her, Luci switched to Larry-Fu stance and bopped a couple of Helena's troops on the head, before performing an elegant, falling down the stairs out of the way of the returning blasts that few past her position.

A little distance away from Luci, Suzie fished out a box that you stick swords into (its technical name) from her cape, dived inside and pulled the swords inside, seemingly committing some kind of magic based Hari Kari on the battlefield. Four of Helena's elite guard approached the box cautiously to work out what happened. As they got right up close, the box collapsed on all sides flattening the troops. Suzie appeared thirty feet from the scene and instinctively gave a little curtsey.

Luci danced over to her side, spinning out of the way of the shots coming her way "you got a ladder in that hat?" she asked, "I could do some real damage with that."

"Lemme see!" Suzie called back whipping her hat off and feeling around "this do?" she pulled out a set of three steps as commonly used in libraries to reach the slightly smutty books.

"I'll improvise it!" Luci yelled over the battlefield noise, an enormous smirk across her face. She took the steps from Suzie's grasp, winked and wheeled away once more into combat. Suzie produced some heavy interlocking rings and whirled them around her head and prepared to engage the three soldiers approaching her flank.

Jane was watching the battle unfold from the back. More accurately, twenty five metres behind the back as far away from those she'd ask to engage in combat as possible (she had gained this tactic from researching British military history and the approach employed by the Generals in what Earth called World War One). Whilst seeing the ebb and flow of battle playing out, she noticed a robed figure stroll jauntily towards her.

Zed and Jane came face to face, or as near as height discrepancies allowed. The two eyed each other up, in Zed's case it was more of a one eye as the saturation in alcohol had somewhat disrupted his focus, neither wanting to make the first move, for fear of revealing they didn't actually know what the first move was, eventually Jane broke the inaction "thumb war?".

"Verily" the bearded figure responded brightly "drink first?" and so saying he produced a flask from within some fold or other in his robes. From another fold he produced a couple of fine glasses and finally, from within a deeper pocket, he produced a fold out standing table. He draped part of his cowl over his arm a la a stereotypical waiter pose. He poured two glasses of bio-fluorescent liquid and took a hefty draft from the nearest glass. Jane followed the mystics lead and took a huge swig. It tasted like a cyborg lemurs piss (and Jane should know), but it had a certain something and that certain something was causing Janes body to do badly co-ordinated internal somersaults.

The stranger extended his hand and Jane followed suit their fingers locking and a frission passed. Jane's brow furrowed as she started to concentrate on the battle of wills that was about to begin.

"One, two, free, four, I declare a thumb war..."

****

Helena stared at the panel in front of her as the moon hit the column. She saw the indentation in it and sighed "I'm sure someone must have commented on how stupid this is" She muttered to herself and lowered her space pants and sat down. The moon really had hit the column at this point.

A noise started, firstly a low murmur building to a loud aggressive hum, like an informant wasp telling his mates where there to find a picnic with a particularly strong artisan bread and preserves selection. The column started to vibrate, Helena gripped the side of the panel as a nervous reflex. A whirring noise started next to her, Helena spun to see a column rising to her right a glass case coming from the floor opening like a petal revealing a rubber glove (pink flavour) which radiated power (or it might just have been clever lighting and dry ice) inside from the glass casing.

Helena allowed herself a moment of quiet triumph and two moments of loud triumph "Huzzah!" she bellowed and punched the air like only Judd Nelson can. She reached for the glove.

"Yoink!" came the shout as Alex appeared from behind the column and snatched the glove before Helena could grasp it.

"Where the flipping, flip did you flipping come from you flip?! How did you get up here?!" Helena yelled enraged.

"Wasn't easy!" Alex replied.

"Why aren't you dead?" Helena demanded.

"I'm not prepared to discuss this with you right now." Alex retorted.

"Are you going to keep quoting lines from 20th century TV shows and films you like?" Helena asked not unreasonably, fixing Alex with a mean stare.

"Your problem" Alex started "Is you want instant gratification. Alex concluded the sermon.

"Meaning?" Helena sneered standing up.

"You took the lift in your hurry to be up here."

"I was in a rush for world domination." Helena reasoned.

"Well if you'd took the time to look, you'd know a staircase runs around the width of the column and I merely dropped a couple of feet onto it when I stepped over the edge." Alex concluded their explanation.

"In the end, it doesn't matter." Helena stated, "I just get the pleasure of killing you myself." Helena caught herself. "Apologies for the hackneyed line, I've been stuck in space for some time, not had much chance to practice speaking to actual people." And with that she lunged forward grasping for the glove.

What followed was a surprisingly high-quality fight for two people with their trousers around their ankles (why neither of them has sought to pull them up at any point is beyond comprehension or explanation).

****

On the battlefield below, having reduced the ladder to splinters from vigorous use, Luci had a troop in an elaborate headlock, another soldier slowly approached. Luci risked a glance up, the trooper took a tentative step towards this slapstick whirling dervish. Luci held up a hand, the trooper instinctively flinched. No wait, look!" Luci instructed pointing up.

"You really expect me to fall for that?!" the soldier grunted.

"Look!" Luci shouted, the soldier looked up at the battle raging above for the glove. Luci cuffed him on the back of the head for good measure and to teach him not to be complacent.

All around the battlefield, combat ceased as everyone started to watch the fight unfurl above them. Zed pulled some popcorn (salted caramel flavour – the animal) from his robes and offered it to Jane who gratefully accepted.

****

Alex ripped themselves from Helena's grasp and found time to pull their pants up. Helena lunged again, sending Alex off balance and the glove came from their grasp flapping towards the edge of the platform. Alex ducked away from Helena instinctively rolling and trapping the glove as the moon beam hit it causing a slight glow to radiate from the glove.

"So close!" Helena goaded managing to free the blaster that had got wrapped in the trousers down by her ankles. "But not close enough." She had Alex in her sights and wasn't going to miss, she squeezed the trigger ready to finally rid herself of this irritating human, but at the last her aim was thrown by the low flying giant space bat returning home miserable after being jilted by the albatross[90]. The bolt flew a foot (with six toes) past Alex.

Alex knew it was now or never. Hurriedly they put the glove on. A kaleidoscope of colours instantly assailed their vision, power coursed

---

[90] Plenty more fish in the sea Mr giant space bat. Actually, that line probably works better for the albatross here.

through Alex's veins, information loaded their brain, tantalising them with all that was, that wasn't and that could be. It was intoxicating, it was all consuming, it was exhilarating, it was, it was, it was…tedious. The information overloading Alex's brain caused them to stumble and fall to the floor. Pain shot up their side as they felt something hard in the pocket of their coat jab into their side as they landed.

Helena stepped closer her gun trained on the prone and struggling Alex.

Alex reached in their pocket for the source of the pain. They felt something small and hard, realising they had the wrong pocket and the cheese and pickle sandwich was now totally beyond redemption Alex quickly reached into their other pocket. Their hand closed round the pocket knife the stranger had given them earlier.

"Thank you stranger, whoever you were!" Alex howled still smarting from the fall and all the information of the universe beaming directly into their brain, but mostly from the fall.

"I was clearly a version of you!" The strangers voice rang in Alex's head. "Honestly we're such an idiot." The stranger signed off with.

Helena started to squeeze the trigger, wishing her gun instructor had been more blasé about her just popping of shots rather than saying she had to always squeeze the trigger.

Wasting no more time, Alex opened the pen knife, the moon glinting off the blade as Alex tore into the glove hacking it to pieces part by part, shards falling on the platform base.

"Nooooo!" cried Helena, dropping her gun putting her hands to her head and falling to the to her knees in reflex. The Moon bored of its bystander role drifted off in search of chocolate based refreshments and crumpets, as the platform started to whirr again and it began lowering itself to the ground, seeming to sense its part in this adventure was done.

The platform hit the floor. Luci and Suzie ran to Alex's side. After initially running in the opposite direction, Zed made his way over and the four went to do a break, but realising they'd not practiced it any further since the abortive attempt outside the Co-Op, so settled instead for a group hug.

Helena pushed herself from her knees and went to where the remnants of the glove lay. Finding an intact finger part, she placed the digit on her finger and pointed at Alex. The finger flew off and farted around the sky like a deflating balloon.

"Noooooo!" said Helena, which was becoming something of a mantra these past few moments. "I only wanted the power patriarchy denies me!". Jane walked over and put a consoling arm around Helena, Helena squeezed back.

Unseen, two figures pushed themselves through the milling troops, who had decided now was a good time for a tea break. The figures reached the side of the now grounded platform. "the human destroyed the glove with the knife and in doing so prevented anyone from gaining the full power of the universe and thus saving the world. They fulfilled the prophecy." Said the High Chamberlain.

"That is exactly what happened Stuart." Said the master archivist.

"Our work here is done." declared the high chamberlain. The two turned and went to seek the Kayak they'd left floating in the river Mersey somewhere hoping some scallies hadn't TWOKed it.

Chapter happen t'her – The Equaliser

A robed figured approached the prostrate Helena and Jane. "My lady, I could not help but note your predicament regarding your gender being a preventative power in you gaining sovereign rule over your planet and loyal territories. The gender equality, or lack thereof, practiced on some planets in this vast universe astonishes and irritates me in equal measure, and I have made a solemn pledge to use all the considerable powers I possess to ensure equality always reigns in these realms. Eth." Zed began "Ergo, I may be able to help you with your difficult circumstances", and so saying he reached into his robes and produced a scroll of paper. "Ah yes, here we are, the laws of the planet Iccles."

"Eccles." Jane corrected him.

"Ah yes," Zed said rolling the paper back up and putting it down his trousers. He produced another rolled parchment from another pocket which he unspooled and preceded to read. "Yikes tis is complicated. Needlessly complicated! I mean, why would you have a rule covering that, it seems so unnecessary and liable to lead to endless boring debate…" Zed spoke, his voice rising a notch "…Oh no that's the offside rule in football." Finally Zed reached into his hood and produced another paper "Ah yes, succession laws on Planet Eccles," Zed started to read the document, eyebrows moving up and down with each word. "Ah yes, flimsy, very flimsy and illegal under the

Youropeeing laws. Did Eccles learn nothing from its seven-thousand-year battle with Yourope? I take it the planet Eccles now has running water again after the debacle of thinking it wanted nothing to do with them?" Zed didn't' wait for a response "Doesn't matter. Anyway, I'll put you in touch with my legal partner Mr Duck, he's the best in the universe with this sort of thing and will have you in power in no time!" Zed clicked is fingers and with a flash and a puff of smoke a business card was in his hand. Zed handed the card to Helena and proceeded to blow on his painful smoking fingers.

Helena smiled "Thank you beardy!" she turned to Jane "come let's go celebrate. There is a pangalactic Tiny Cook on the way home that does a meal so greasy you get to spend the next four days sliding around on your belly."

"I'm in!" squealed Jane. And with that the two of them bounced off Jane helping Helena finally pull her pants back up.

The rest of the troops seeing them dance off shrugged and followed. Hoping to get home in time to watch re-runs of Live at the Apollo.

Zed returned to his three companions who again embraced joyously at their victory.

Chapter 57 – to the victors the Curlywurly

Alex was feeling really pleased with themselves. Almost as pleased as the time they nearly managed to belch the 'Crimewatch UK' theme music. Although that life milestone was always going to take some beating, and saving the entire world from tyranny just wasn't quite up there.

Alex became aware of a presence behind them spinning to find themselves face to face with Claire. "Impressive!" Claire started "Your ability to screw up and break everything saved the day. I always knew you had it in you!"

"You saw that?" Alex started surprised before catching themselves "Hey you know I meant to break that glove, right?!"

Claire deliberately ignored the second part of Alex's sentence. "A fight for the fate of the galaxy? Yeah course I saw it, it was on News North West, just after an item about a pensioner who talks to hens. I came down to offer your hearty congratulations." She offered Alex her hand and gave a firm handshake before pulling them in for a hug.

"Want to come with me for a drink in Sale sometime?" Alex asked flushed.

"Of course not." Claire winked "But the transport network runs to other locations you know." She smiled at Alex over her shoulder as she walked off.

High overhead the park, Brandon The Brontosaur pulled up his jetpack to hover mode and foresaw the scene playing out below. Steph the Stegosaur pulled up alongside him. "What now Brandon? Do we swoop in and save humankind?"

"Err, no, looks like we're a little late and it's all in hand. I knew we shouldn't have stopped for that salad sandwich and overprice latte at the Babylon 4 Services".

"Ah well, we tried to help" Steph said philosophically, "I hear they've got Laser Quest just up the road. Fancy that?" Brandon nodded and the two kicked their jet packs into 'go fast in a direction' mode and made their way.

"Nicely done eh Suzie?" Luci smiled backing up to survey the wreckage as the last of the troops left the field rubbing bruises and Chinese burns. Luci took another step back and her heel stepped against something large and squishy.

"Careful now!" boomed a voice with a slight Welsh twinge. Luci spun and in alarm saw a twenty foot tall snail with an armoured helmet which its inquisitive eyes reached out of, scanning the scene in front, and a little behind. Behind him, her (it?) was a legion of similar sized snails all dressed in heavy plate armour.

"Sorry!" was the best Luci could manage, she'd seen a lot these last few days, but she just wasn't prepared for a conversation with giant armoured molluscs. Which was a shame as she was usually pretty good at that kind of thing. The lead snail's eyes swivelled and fixed on the horn around Luci's neck.

"What is thy bidding master?" The snail asked bowing its head slightly "Whatever your enemy, we will crush it wholly, or partly if you prefer, it's your call really, we're open to suggestions."

Luci raised her eyebrow "Without wishing to be unoriginal." Luci began "but…sorry?!".

"The horn of Bob Holness Blockbusters!" the snail boomed back its tone almost reverential. "You are its keeper and us your willing servants".

"Oh yeah, that. I blew that ages ago when I needed help fighting a robot, but now…" Luci saw the snails eyebrows shoot up. This was especially disconcerting as it didn't have eyebrows. Luci could see the inevitable 'we got here as quick as we could' line about to be delivered by the snail and changed tact "…thanks for coming to check all is OK, that's very kind of you. I think we're all good now so why don't you take the day off? Have some rest and relaxation?"

"Good news lads and lasses!" The snail bellowed over its shoulder "we can go pitch and putting!" and to general mirth the snails turned and left. Their voices trailing off, sort of, not really their slow progress and loud voices meant everyone heard their conversation playing out.

Luci soon found herself flanked by Alex Suzie and Zed.

"Well we did it! Never in doubt, I always knew working together we would" Suzie declared breezily.

"You watch my first tee shot Barry, it will be amazing!" A voice cut across.

"Hang on" Luci said to Suzie tapping her on the arm, before shouting over her shoulder "Can you departing snails keep it down slightly please? We've some important dialogue going on here. I think…"

"Sorry!" A voice boomed from really not far away at all.

"The galaxy is free from the tyranny of misuse of the all-powerful glove. Truly an act of heroism occurred here today" Alex declared with no small degree of smugness.

"Are you sure you're not one of those Expositiongonians, or whatever they're called?" Luci asked Alex sarcastically. Alex stared at Luci blankly "never mind.".

"What now?" Alex asked looking around at the park.

Suzie looked at each of her companions and smiled "Well we've proven we're a fearsome outfit for those that would wish the universe ill. But evil never sleeps, it just sets its alarm for snooze, so further dangers will present themselves soon enough. So, we need to be ready for the next challenge that awaits." She stared into the distance for a moment "the paperwork for this is one going to be a bugger for me though. I'll send it to my PA though."

Alex looked directly at Suzie "no I mean what immediately now?".

"Pubeth?" Zed interjected enthusiastically.

"I know loads of shit pubs!" Alex spoke triumphantly. The four nodded at each other, linked arms and made their way to the park gate.

"'Sake!" Alex wailed looking at their foot, "As if I haven't had enough of them to last me a lifetime, I've just stepped in another dog turd!" then catching themselves, "nothing a pint won't resolve!". With that the four picked up the pace and exited through the gate.

From behind them where Alex had slipped a whirring started up, the ground began to shake and a large column started to rise from the ground.

"I'm going to write to the council to check the deeds on these things!" a resident angrily bellowed over a hedge into the empty park.

Chapter Nearly There – In the Beginning (or at least pretty close to the beginning, in all honesty this chapter is probably in totally the wrong place) there was a word. And that word was glove.

Valhar The Creator, daughter of Albess The Creator of The Creator and Jacelen The Co-creator of the Creator who in turn were the children of Tigarch The Creator, Creating The Creator and…Looks let's just say their family tree is more of an aggressively expanding forest.

Start again.

Valhar The Creator looked at the glove she had created laid out on her workbench. It was a little rudimentary in appearance. Using a washing glove up with a few leads and a bit of glitter to give it sparkle she had created, something of limited interest. However, it was the chip of Coughcoughahem she had created that gave the wearer the power over the whole universe that made this glove especially nifty. She was hoping this would get her a B+ in her school design project. She wasn't optimistic though, as the self-sustaining sun she had built had only received a somewhat disappointing C.

The glove was to run on Lunar power (as Valhar wanted to do her bit for the environment in the universe), but which moon? Valhar reached for Encyclopaedia Universica. Flipping the pages and dropping her finger she came across Luna Selene AKA The Moon that orbited a distant primitive backwater called Earth. 'Yeah that'll do' she thought to herself.

Realising she didn't want the power kicking in straight away (ultimate power ideally should have a cooling off period), she built in a protective device so that The Moon would only be able to power it 10,000,000,000 years in the future hence, that seemed a reasonable amount of time for a person to decide if they really want the whole power of the universe. Valhar accepted that the inability to demonstrate the glove in action immediately might drop her a mark or two from the teacher.

Pleased with the concept, Valhar went to see her mum and dad to ask if she could have tea and biscuits before her evening meal.

Stainton, The Chaos Bringer (talk about nominative determinism) snuck from behind the curtain where he had been watching his sister Valhar work. He jauntily crossed to her workbench, pulled on the glove and flexed his fingers. He pointed at Valhars terrapin tank and clicked his fingers. Nothing. Unusually for Stainton he looked at the instructions (not really the forte of a chaos bringer). He read the part about the glove taking 10,000,000,000 years to power up, he didn't really have time for that. He really wanted to get on with watching his favourite boxed set 'Frollicks in the Big Town'. "Bah!" He said theatrically. Removing the glove and stuffing it in his pocket he left Valhars room, descending the stairs and making his way to the utility room.

He reached the rubbish shoot, placed the glove in and set the shoot to blast the glove randomly into out of space, region unknown. Pleased with his work, he made his way to the kitchen to ask his mum and dad if he could get tea and biscuits before his evening tea.

****

When Valhar found out about Stainton and the glove she hit the roof, but it was no use, she couldn't find the glove up there. So instead she went and moaned to her mum and dad. Albess and Jacelen being reasonable and forward-thinking parents made Stainton write a novel explaining where he'd gone wrong and hypothesising what may have happened to the glove. Stainton did as he was told, and this book went on to become a top selling self-help book for deluded idiots across the universe. To this date it can regularly be found at airport shops and space docking stations.

Jacelen and Albess knew the glove was a potential threat to the entire universe, but they did not panic too much knowing they had 10,000,000,000 years to find it. So, they wrote to their Local Intergalactic Authority to report it missing. By the time the letter made it to the appropriate person at the council it was 9,789 years before the gloves power would be able to be utilised.

Upset at this turn of events, Valhar decided she would also get rid of the fully working prototype of the glove she had created and kept separately from the lost glove. She also fired that into the space via the rubbish shoot.

She decided to make a start on her book 'Designing Things for the Galaxy Isn't Fair When Your Parents Don't Understand You.' This was ultimately turned into a tedious musical by a former firebrand stand-up comedian, come mainstream sell out, in partnership with a bloated space Toad. It ran for a depressingly long time on the West End of Londononium 7.

100 years from power up date, the Local Authority had got the paperwork to search for the glove signed off. And a week later they found the main glove and were pretty confident they knew where the other one may be. The council wrote to Valhar to see if she wanted it back, but Valhar had washed her hands of it, which would have been difficult to do if she was wearing the glove.

The council convened a meeting to decide what to do with the glove when it reached it power up state in 6 months' time. Swift action was needed it would have to go to the quarterly all council meeting or something. In the meantime, they gave the gloves to Odin the office junior to see if he had any ideas what to do with it.

Postscript:

Valhar ultimately submitted a CD wrack for her design project, gaining a C+ in the process. Design teachers love a CD wrack[91].

---

[91] The digitalization of music really does threaten the backup plan of every lazy design student out there.

Epilogue

Barry had reached the end of reading his book on the toilet. Truly it had been an epic log.

He strolled down his ship's corridor, descending the nice wooden staircase he'd had installed and stepped into his control room at the bottom. "Aye up love!" he called to Lindsey, who had decided it was such a long journey she wanted to change her name from Zule as it was something to do. He sat in his command chair, helpfully aided by the fact Lindsey had stuck a post it note with 'command chair' written on it over the crude biro labelling of Barry.

Barry surveyed the command panel in front of him, he compared the levers and checked the light readings, it was no use though, he didn't know what any of the big displays meant. A red light with a mushroom cloud suddenly blinked furiously at Barry. "Lindsey, t'croissants are ready!" he yelled in shock even though Lindsey's chair was three foot away.

"I think Barry" Lindsey began in soothing tones "that light is telling us we've reached our destination; planet Earth." Before adding diplomatically "I'll check the croissants too.".

Barry reached for a leaver and wound down the window, As the Flying Gerbil descended, he saw they were landing on a gassy fireball with no discernible signs of life. "Earth. And if I'm not very much mistaken, Barnsley!" Barry boomed cheerfully.

Lindsey smiled and nodded as she primed the escape pod for herself.

Barry chucked "It hasn't changed one bit!".

The Solicitor Duck will return in his own adventure.

About the author

Olly is a vaguely pointless sort of Terran from a drab suburb in Manchester (any similarities with locations in the book are entirely coincidentally deliberate). If he has seen further than others, its because he poked them in the eye with a stick.

When not knocking out poorly conceived, stories puns and poems and subjecting the world to them on his blog, he likes to stare moodily out of the window listening to self indulgent electro and ambient music or meet friends and family. Preferably the latter.

He has been known to struggle with thE CAPS Lock and would like the world to just kind of, you know, try and get on, show tolerance, be excellent to each other and party on. This is his first book, but he's liable to churn out more shit if you're not careful.

Printed in Great Britain
by Amazon